FRANKENSTEIN
MONSTERS OF THE ABYSS

John L. French   Patrick Thomas

PADWOLF PUBLISHING INC.
WWW.PADWOLF.COM
www.facebook.com/Padwolf

www.theagentsoftheabyss.com

FRANKENSTEIN: MONSTERS OF THE ABYSS
by
John L. French and Patrick Thomas
© 2021 Patrick Thomas

cover by Patrick Thomas

Agents of the Abyss created by Patrick Thomas and all related characters and settings are © and ™ Patrick Thomas

ISBN 978-1-890096-95-3
FIrst Printing.

*Dedicated to the memory of R. Allen Leider.
Rick, you'll be missed.*

Memo from Abraham Van Helsing, Founder and Lord Protector of the Sway

The Monster that fancied himself a man was among the greatest individual threats to human purity, second only to the malevolent Transylvanian count who eventually fancied himself a king.

The monster's telling of how he came to be must never be released to the populace least it deceive true humans into thinking him anything less than a pitiable beast, a monster not fit to live among us, worthy only of scorn and death.

Instead allow the release of his maker's version. Lies though they be, their message better fit with the mission of the Sway to destroy the monsters and protect the human bloodline.

He was conceived in the mind of a madman. He was shaped by the flesh and bones of the dead. He was birthed on a table in the room of his father. He was brought to life by the storm.

Abandoned by his maker, he sought the dark places. His school was the deep woods. His friends – he had none. His family – best not to ask.

He was hated and reviled, blamed for crimes that he claimed he did not commit.

He had no name. He was never given one. He was Adam and Satan. He was Creature and Monster, Demon and Killer. He was thought to be the spawn of the Devil, and this may have been correct.

Call him as we know him. Call him after the one who created him. Call him:

Frankenstein.

1

"But Alphonse, why? Why must I leave?"

"Because, Sister, your condition, well, it is a disgrace to House Frankenstein. A discrete dalliance is one thing, but in a few months, things will not be so … discrete. Which is why it is best you leave now. I have arranged a villa for you … and the child at Lake Como. It is there, as the widow Lavenza, you will bear and raise your bastard. Or give it away. Or drown it in the lake. I care not. But from here on, you and it are no longer part of this house. Farewell, Emily. This is the last time we shall speak."

Dearest Caroline,

Please forgive my writing to you. I pray that you have done well over the last four years and that you do not throw this letter into the fire as I suspect Alphonse has done with those I have written him. I write not for myself but for my daughter, Elizabeth. She is, as you know, just four years old. She is a beautiful child, one whom any house would be proud of. The situation here in Lake Como is dire. I am ill with the fever and likely to die. It may be that by the time this letter reaches your hand I will already be in the Hands of the Lord, if He has so willed it. If that is so, I beg you to take in my sweet Elizabeth, whose only crime was to be born to a mother who let her passions lead her into a sinful liaison. Should my time come, I will place her with a family in the town, leaving a sum of money for her care. These people are of peasant stock, but honest and hard-working and will raise Elizabeth as their own if you are unable to persuade Alphonse to take her into his care. But I beg of you, when you married my brother, I welcomed you, called you "sister," and loved you as one. I believe that love was returned to me by you. For this love we once shared, do not abandon Elizabeth, but take her in and raise her, if not as your daughter, then as your niece.

May God bless you and count you as one of His Chosen.

Emily Lavenza, formerly of House Frankenstein.

"I thought I made our position on this matter clear years ago, Caroline."

"You made *your* position clear, Alphonse. As you recall, I did not share it. All I did was yield to yours as a good wife should."

"I see nothing in this letter to change my mind."

"No, Alphonse. Then perhaps you should read it again. You know that I have always prayed for a daughter but despite our many attempts, pleasant as they were, the Lord has not yet blessed us with another child. This letter, this cry for help from she who we both at one time called *Sister* may be His way of answering my prayers. We could say that she was the child of Milanese nobles, a child we rescued from poverty and adopted into our House. To her we would 'Uncle' and 'Aunt.' To Victor, she would be 'Cousin.' To him, she would be a playmate and companion, and maybe more when the time comes."

"I do not know, Caroline."

"Then you would condemn your own blood, to be raised by … peasants? I thought you a better man, Alphonse Frankenstein."

Alphonse Frankenstein sighed. He was the head of House Frankenstein, a landowner, and a member of the Genevan Council. He oversaw a great and prosperous estate with many servants and was esteemed by his colleagues and peers. And yet, he could never win an argument with his wife over something about which she was truly determined.

He had heard the Lord's Word preached. He had read His book several times, in several translations. "Wives, obey your husbands as you obey the Lord," Ephesians said. Not for the first time did he think that somewhere in the past there had been a mistranslation, and he was sure that he understood why, when He had walked this Earth, the Lord had not married.

"Very well, my dear Caroline, let us travel to Como and adopt this 'Milanese orphan.' But you must swear to me that you will never reveal to her the truth of her birth, or that she is, by blood, a Frankenstein."

"Of course, husband."

2

The storm came upon them suddenly. It was violent and angry, the worst Victor Frankenstein had ever seen, the worst his father could remember. The weather's fury drew him. While everyone else huddled for safety inside the house, Victor stood on the balcony of his room, watching the lightning and listening to the thunder. He could hear the cries of the animals over the noise of the rain – their shrieks of terror, their cries of death. Some dared to leave the woods and come into the clearing, only to run back to what until that night had been a place of safety.

A glow in the distance, somewhere the forest was burning. Victor knew that for what it was, nature's way of renewal, like the Phoenix's death by fire followed by regeneration and new life.

If only, he thought, *that worked in other ways. That we could be renewed, that the lightning could be called down and bring us, bring them* back.

A maid came in. "Your father wishes you to join the family, Master Victor."

"Thank you, Clarice. Please tell my father that if the storm shifts, I will do so. But for now, I am safe where I am. Wet, but safe."

"Perhaps later the master will need to be dried off," she said with a certain smile, which Victor returned.

"Perhaps," But he knew he wouldn't. Clarice was one of his father's special maids, one with duties that went beyond housekeeping. He knew that his father had used her and maybe one or two others on occasions when his wife Caroline, Victor's mother, would not invite him into her chamber. He used them even more now that his mother was dead. And his father made it clear that Victor was free to do so as well.

"That's what they're for, Victor," Alphonse had told him. Victor knew that Clarice would be willing to help him take that last step from boy to man, but Victor was not willing. Nor had he succumbed to the not so veiled hints from his friend Henry Clerval. He and the merchant's son had been as close as brothers since they met in the woods, the same woods that now might burn this night. They played in some old ruins which at times became a castle and at others a ship. They played at pirates and knights, sometimes involving Victor's golden-haired cousin Elizabeth when they needed a princess to capture or save, or a damsel to rescue.

Elizabeth sometimes played those roles, but as often or not she'd choose a branch or stick for her sword and fight dragons and villains alongside them.

They got older and changed as they did. Elizabeth became a young lady whose duties and station did not permit her to slay dragons. Victor grew hair and he felt urges that his father explained to him then told him of the maids. Victor was not interested. Nor was he interested when Henry told him where his interests lay. At his friend's first proposition, Victor declined but did not shun his friend as others might. Henry was, Victor decided, as the Lord made him and so his nature and desires were between the two of them.

The lightning flashed brighter, the thunder crack louder and faster. The storm was coming closer, the rain coming down harder.

I might have to have Clarice dry me off anyway, he thought with a smile. *And if her hand strays I might let it. But only that.*

Yes, only that. Other than that, he would keep his body pure. Pure for Elizabeth. Elizabeth, whom his parents had adopted in Milan, who had been a "gift" from his mother. He had treated her as his gift, treating her as he did the puppies and kittens he had played with. One day he pushed her, and she pushed back. He pushed harder and she curled her fist and hit him in the stomach. His first lesson, his father told him, on how to treat a lady and what might happen if one did not properly learn said lesson.

Now that Elizabeth was a young woman, it was understood by all that one day they would be wed. Victor often thought of their marriage, and of Elizabeth as his bride, and early on he vowed to remain pure until he was with her on their wedding night.

More lightning, closer thunder. Soon his father would come himself and drag Victor away. But until then he would stand and marvel.

Just then there was a flash and a crack all at once. Victor looked out and saw that the old oak tree was no more, that Jupiter had voiced his rage and sent his bolt to reduce it to a smoldering stump.

Such power. Did the power to destroy also mean the power to create? He had read nothing about this in his study of the old natural scientists, philosophers, and alchemists. Neither Cornelius Agrippa, Paracelsus, Albertus Magnus, nor even Isaac Newton had mentioned the lightning in their quest to look into the Abyss as they searched for the Philosopher's Stone or the Elixir of Life.

Victor did not care about turning lead into gold, but the other … How many times did he wish he could bring someone or something back from the final darkness?

When he was too young to know what he was doing, he had played roughly with a puppy. As it lay lifeless on the ground he demanded of the servants, and then of his parents, "Bring it back!"

Of course, no one could. This was to be his first experience, but hardly his last, with death. And even at his young age, he could not help but wonder if there was not a way to return the departed to life.

There had been a maid. She had been given charge over him while he played. She looked away for just a moment. Time enough for him to take a fall, tear his clothes, and gash his knee on a sharp rock. (He still bore the scar.) That night there were cries and screams and not just from him. The unfortunate woman was not seen again, not in Geneva, nor perhaps anywhere else.

"Bring her back!" he demanded of his father, for Victor had liked the older girl who sometimes gave him sweets.

"Yes, Alphonse, bring her back," his mother had said in a tone his father had never heard her use.

"That is not possible," his father said sharply, then left the room. Later he heard his parents arguing and later idly noticed that his father had not visited his mother's chambers for a fortnight, although at the time he did not realize the significance of this.

His mother. It still pained him to think of her sacrifice.

His cousin had grown ill with Scarlet Fever.

"Do not take her," Victor had shouted from his balcony, imploring a God who, according to the Calvinist minster, had already determined everyone's fate in this world and the next.

Nursed by his mother, his beloved cousin lived. But in tending to her niece, Caroline contracted the fever. "Do not take her," Victor again cried to the heavens. But this time his prayers, if heard, were not answered. On the day his mother died, he went out on the balcony only to curse the name of an unfeeling God he no longer believed existed.

"Victor, come away from the storm, Son."

Victor thought to refuse but knew it would do him no good. "Yes, Father." Leaving the storm behind, he dried himself off, dressed in fresh clothing, and joined his family for dinner. And as he ate, thoughts of the storm, the power of lightning, and of the Phoenix ran through his mind.

It would never truly stop its mad race.

3

It was a month after his mother's death that Victor left for Ingolstadt to attend its university. When his carriage arrived, everyone turned out to witness his departure and to bid him farewell. His brother Ernest was the first. Victor's junior by seven years, it seemed that his body was trying to outgrow its youthfulness and all he seemed to talk about was joining the Guard when he was of age.

"It's action for me, Victor," he had said more than once. "You study and be smart. I'll fight and be brave."

"I'm sure you will, Ernest."

Their brother William was the youngest of the family. He had been born just before Elizabeth had taken ill with the fever that had taken his mother. He was brought out to see his oldest brother off by his nanny, Justine Moritz.

Justine was another of what Alphonse called his wife's strays. When Lady Frankenstein died, the care of her youngest son fell to his nanny. Justine was a young girl from Geneva whose mother had neither the means nor the inclination to care for her or her siblings. Justine did the best that she could for them until the fever took them as well. When Caroline heard of her plight, she supported the young girl first with funds and when she was orphaned took her into the household. She had wanted to adopt the child but Alphonse refused, stating that her low birth made her unfit to bear the name Frankenstein. Instead, Justine became a favored servant, devoted to Caroline. It was she who nursed the woman who was more of a mother to her than her own through her illness and, when the end was near, it was to her that Lady Frankenstein entrusted the care of William.

"Be the mother to him that the Lord would not permit me to be."

"I will, Madame. I swear it by the Cross."

"Goodbye, Master Victor," Justine said, holding William up to him.

Victor took his youngest brother in his arms, hugged him, and give him back to Justine.

"Take good care of him, Justine. Tell him of our mother." Then *sotto voce*, added, "And do not be alone with my father."

She nodded and whispered back. "I know, your mother, rest her soul, warned me against him, as did Clarice and some other girls."

Henry was there as well. The two friends shook hands.

"Good luck, Victor. With luck, I'll be able to convince my father to let me join you in a year or two. Until then, stay out of trouble. At least until I'm there to help you get into it." Elizabeth was next. Much to Victor's surprise, she hugged him tight and kissed his lips in a most uncousinly way. "Hurry back to me, Victor. And then …" She left the rest of her farewell unstated, letting her smile and her eyes finish for her.

"Farewell, Elizabeth. Please look after William and Justine. I leave you in Henry's care until my return. You will be safe with him."

"I know." Another smile, as if she had discerned their friend's nature.

As was proper, Alphonse was last. He gripped his son's hand tightly and said, "Would that your mother was here. She would be proud of you, as am I. Work hard, Victor, and bring honor to the name Frankenstein."

"I will, Father."

Victor climbed into the waiting carriage. At seventeen, he was leaving behind his family, friends, and all that he knew. He was scared and excited. A part of him wanted to yell "Halt" and remain home. The rest looked forward to years ahead and the discoveries he might make.

Perhaps he could finally catch up to the phoenix who still raced among his thoughts.

4

*D*ear Henry,

Please forgive my not writing to you for the past several months but the university is much more taxing than I expected. Alone for the first time, there was no one to turn to for help. Fortunately, I found the students' quarter here in Ingolstadt and was able to secure lodgings. They are not in the best area, but as they are the only ones available, I have made do. The residents of the town regard us an unruly lot. I must confess that having met my fellow students, there is a point to their argument.

My lodgings are on the second floor, a climb of several sets of stairs each time. I have a sitting room and a bedroom, plus one more that will make a fine workroom once I can gather the proper equipment.

Securing an apartment was not the greatest of my challenges, however. When I first arrived at the University, I presented my letters of introduction and was led to one M. Krempe, a most disheveled man, uncouth and unshaven, the very opposite of what you and I believed a professor of natural philosophy should be. He immediately dismissed my previous studies of Agrippa, Paracelsus, Magnus, and Newton as a waste of time that is now lost to me, although he did commend the latter's work on mathematics and the studies of physical motion. He claimed that their theories were "exploded systems" and set before me a course of study involving the more "modern" disciplines of chemistry and what he called life science. Having read some of these works it appears that the writers either ignored or discarded a thousand years of thought and research in favor of starting anew. It is if one would tear down a house and reconstruct it rather than build on what is already there while fixing any flaws found.

There is, however, another professor, M. Waldman, who has a differing viewpoint. M. Waldman is also dismissive of the "ancients," as he calls them, stating that they promised miracles but produced nothing. He compares them unfavorably to the modern masters who have revealed the secrets of nature from the microscopic to the heavens, explaining how blood circulates and how the air we breathe gives us life. They have harnessed the lightning and mimicked the earthquake. But later, when we spoke in private, he credited these same ancients not for their achievements but for establishing the foundations on which our modern philosophy is built. If I may return to my analogy of a house, it is as if they had built a shaky house on a good foundation. The old house must be torn down but thanks to their work, a new and stronger one can be constructed using the old design as a starting point..

I think I will be in Ingolstadt longer than planned. I must study the works and results of what I was ignorant. At the same time, I will not abandon those who built the foundation. I feel, and I must confess that I am alone in this, that there is worth in them yet. Maybe it is my foolish pride that causes me to write this, but I believe that I may one day be able to reconcile the old and the new into something wondrous.

Please tell my father, brothers, and my dear Elizabeth that I am doing well and will write to them soon.

Your dear friend,
Victor

5

*D*ear Henry,

    Please express my thanks to my family, especially Elizabeth, for their letters. Assure them that I have not forgotten them, just as I have not forgotten you, although I am sure you have thought otherwise. but that my work here occupies most of my waking hours. Not to mention much of my dreams.

    I am close, Henry, very close. Agrippa, Paracelsus, and the others did not produce because while they were exploring the natural world and trying to go beyond it, they had not the tools. It is difficult to find one's way in the dark without a torch. One cannot build a house (yes, the same house as before) without tools. One cannot prepare a meal without growing or hunting the food. So it was with the ancients. They had the ideas but not the tools with which to pursue them.

    But modern philosophers seem to have the opposite problems. They can watch blood flow, they can create a spark that simulates lightning, they can look into the heavens and count the rings of Saturn, but they know not what to do with their knowledge. They have the tools but no plans on how to build the house. They have a torch to dispel the darkness but no path to follow through the shadows of the world's ignorance. They have food but no recipe and so go hungry when with the right insight could produce a feast the like of which the world has never seen..

    Maybe it is hubris but as I read both old and new and apply one to the other they begin to come together in my mind. I believe that I am about to take the first steps on a great journey. Where it will lead, I know not, nor do I know what awaits my arrival. I fear to start, knowing that once I do, I will never be able to step off the path.

    As always, I remain your dear friend,
Victor

6

The lectures of Augustus Darvell were the most talked-about ones in Ingolstadt, just as M. Darvell was one of the most talked-about professors. Due to a medical condition, Darvell was extremely sensitive to light. Exposure to sunlight caused his skin to blister, his eyes to water, and his head to ache. Those who had visited his chambers reported that he kept his shutters closed and locked and lit just enough candles to provide the minimum of light. Likewise, his lecture hall was kept dark, the only light provided by the *lanterna magica* which he used to project images of his subject matter. Due to his aversion to light of any kind, Darvell's skin was extremely pale, almost translucent, and the man himself was the subject of much talk and speculation.

It was not until Victor had entered his second-year studies that Professors Krempe and Waldman spoke to Victor about his request to attend Darvell's lectures. They praised him for having progressed further than they thought he would in his knowledge of the application of the physical philosophies, for making strides that left his fellow students far behind him.

Unaware that Victor was using the older philosophers as his foundation for his study of the modern, Krempe asked him, "See what can be accomplished when you throw out the old and embrace the new?"

"If that is the case, my dear fellow, it is a wonder that your wife has not left you for a younger man," jibed Waldman.

"Would that it was so, Waldman. That woman is my punishment here on Earth. If belief in witches were permitted, I would swear she was one and tie the noose myself."

"Then why don't you leave her?"

"I don't know. I think the only reason we stay together is that each of us is waiting for the other to die, so we can piss on the other's grave. But Victor here does not need to know of my woes, or yours for that matter. Or the need to repeat them." Krempe cast a bloodshot eye toward his student. "Isn't that so, young man?"

"I'm sorry, sir," Victor said with as much false innocence as he dared. "I was mentally comparing the calculus of Newton to that of Leibniz, wondering which was best to solve a particular problem, and missed your conversation. My apologies to both of you."

Krempe smiled and Waldman openly laughed. "Well said, young man. I see that you are learning more than philosophy," the latter said. "But to the matter at hand. Because of your progress, we have decided to allow you to attend the lectures of Augustus Darvell, for as long as you can. M. Darvell's subject matter, as you are aware, is death and decay. Few students who begin his talks make it through to their end."

"What know you of death, young Frankenstein, that you wish to study it?"

Addressing both men, Victor said, "I have seen death. It has struck my family and friends, and it saddens and frightens me. I wish to study death to ease my grief and confront my fears and, of course, advance my knowledge."

Based on his readings of alchemical texts, Victor had other motives as well, ones he felt he should keep to himself and not share with his professors. They would not approve. Or they judge him mad and the avenues of knowledge they could open might be forever lost.

The two men looked at each other and nodded as well. "Again, well said, Victor," Waldman commented. "Darvell's first lecture is tomorrow night. It will begin just after the sun goes down. You should arrive early so as to find a seat."

"Is it that well attended, Monsieur?"

"No, the room is that dark."

7

The next evening Victor found himself accompanied by some of his fellow students as they walked toward the lecture hall.

"It is said," commented Gaffner, one of their number, "that Darvell is not quite human, that he is one of the undead, a *nosferatu*."

"Where is your proof?" asked Droz, another student. "Have you been to his apartments? Have you seen his coffin full of earth? Has he sucked your blood? Or maybe he sucked something else of yours? That is one way to achieve praise from your professors."

When the laughter died down, Victor said, "It is more likely that M. Darvell suffers from photophobia." As his fellows glared at him for ruining their fun, he added, "Or perhaps he just doesn't foul his own nest, that he leaves the university alone and preys on the villagers."

Good humor restored, Gaffner said, "Someone should. In fact, there are a few of the village girls I'd like to prey on."

"Then you should pray harder for success," quipped Droz.

"Oh, I'm hard enough, I just need the opportunity. The right opening if you will."

And on that, the laughing students entered the darkened hall.

"Let us speak of death," Augustus Darvell said in a slight Slavic accent as he began his lecture, "and what happens to the body afterward. Please note that I said, 'the body.' I will not be discussing what happens to the deceased's spirit once it leaves its mortal shell. That is a subject for men wiser and more learned in scripture than I. No, we will be talking about what changes occur to one's physical form once it is deprived of the spark of life that animates it. If you please, Fritz."

Light from the *lanterna magica* appeared on the white-washed wall behind M. Darvell. Then his large assistant placed the first glass slide into it. An image taken from woodcut and etched into the slide appeared on the wall. It was of a dead body.

"I apologize for the quality of the image. Despite the efforts of de la Roche and Scheele, there is not yet a way to faithfully capture an actual image. It may be that we are not meant to, that the Lord might consider that faithful reproduction of His creation a sin of hubris and lead us to another Babel. But again, I leave matters of belief to those to whom He has called to be shepherds over us."

Slide after slide followed, each one showing as best it could the process of decay and decomposition. Darvell let the images speak for themselves, not speaking until the slide show was over.

"Light more candles, if you please, Fritz. Let us now see each other."

As the room slowly brightened, Darvell said, "It is not true that I am afraid of the light. I enjoy the soft glow of candlelight. It is the harsh rays of the sun that blisters my skin and burns my eyes. And now that matter has been mentioned, it shall not be remarked upon again. What will be discussed in upcoming classes will be the process of decay which you have just witnessed. There will be trips to morgues, charnel houses, and graveyards as well. Yes, a question."

"M. Darvell, will we be permitted to view an autopsy?" asked a student sitting close to Victor.

"No, sir, we will not. While there is no sin in viewing or studying the natural processes, we may not desecrate a body, for it once housed an immortal spirit and so due respect must be paid. And with that, we are done for the night. Please follow the torchbearers back to your quarters and return here after sunset in two days."

Back in his apartment, Victor thought about what M. Darvell has said. There was one phrase to which his mind kept returning – the spark of life that animates the body. It reminded him of passages from Agrippa's occult philosophy and commentaries on Hebraic texts. Paracelsus wrote of an "anima" from which life was born, and Newton speculated on a cause of generation.

If, Victor wondered, this "spark of life" animates a body when it is first born then would it be possible, for another, different kind of "spark," possibly the elixir of life which Newton sought, to animate a body after death? If so, that meant that death need not be forever and that new life could be created from the old.

Victor Frankenstein did not sleep that night. Instead, he thought of those he had lost – his pets, the maid who screamed and cried in the night, his sainted mother. "Bring them back!" he had prayed and demanded. But his prayers had not been answered nor were his demands met. The phoenix slowed its eternal race long enough to whisper, "Not then, but maybe soon."

§

For months, Victor studied the dead. From M. Darvell he learned the process of decay. The theory of spontaneous generation and whether flies and maggots were attracted to dead bodies or arose from them was discussed, debated, and disproved experimentally. There were the promised visits. The morgues gave the students their first close-up look at death undisguised by Frederik Ruysch's embalming techniques. For a handful of coins, the attendants would set a corpse aside and the class would visit time after time to observe the process. Those who did not sicken, or who did not find the process of death disturbing then went to the charnel houses, where the bones of the dead were stored once removed from their graves to make room for more of their fellows. Along the way, the students, accompanied by the oddly cheerful Darvell, would pass through the cemeteries, the ones with family crypts where the bodies of the dead might lie for all eternity without fear that their rest would be disturbed by the gravedigger's pick and shovel.

By the time Darvell was finishing his lecture series, there were but a handful of students remaining. Many dropped out – those who curiosity was more than satisfied, those whose dreams were haunted by corpses rising from the dead, and those who took offense that Darvell required more than their mere attendance – that they were expected to read, discuss, and participate in the handling and examination of bones of various animals. Two were ejected from the class, one for the removal of souvenirs from a charnel house and the other for the unnatural fondling of a female corpse. He was turned over to church authorities and was not again seen in Ingolstadt.

Victor was one of those who remained. Each night he would learn something new. He would then return to his rooms where he was unable to sleep until he found corresponding passages in the tomes that his mentors did not know he still possessed and read. Sometimes there were none, the old science not up to the new. Sometimes the books went beyond Darvell's teachings, with descriptions and woodcuts of the body's interior. He longed for a closer look, to see firsthand the fullness of the Lord's creation and what wonders were inside the human body.

In class, they had dissected the lower animals – rats, and rabbits, and other small game. One night there was a dog, a sickly one that had to be put down. A few coins and Darvell took the animal away with him. There was also a pig. M. Darvell did not state where that was obtained.

But no human corpse could be so desecrated this way. Church fathers and elders, both Calvinist and Catholic, kept a close watch on Darvell's activities. They had heard the rumors, heard Darvell referred to as ghoul, fiend, and even vampyre. But as distasteful as his subject matter was, they found that neither it nor he violated any laws set down by the Bible or either church.

As far as they knew.

It was near the end of the term when Darvell called out to Victor as the young man was leaving.

"Frankenstein, a word please before you go."

"Yes, Monsieur, what is it?"

"Do not take what I say amiss, Victor, but I have noticed that you are … comfortable around the dead."

"It is not so much comfort as the realization that the dead cannot hurt me unless I am foolish enough to forget your safety warnings."

"It is more than that, Victor, is it not?"

"Yes, Monsieur, it is. I wish to learn all of life's secrets, and to know them, I must also learn all of death's secrets as well. I only wish… but no, never mind."

"Is it just the two of here, Victor," Darvell said quietly, stepping close to the young man. At first, Victor thought that the professor had the same tastes as did his friend Henry and was prepared to reject him gently while vowing to keep his secret. But instead, Darvell said in a whispered voice that only Victor could hear, "What is it that you wish?"

"We have looked into the bodies of the smaller animals, but I wish I could see inside the body of man, to know how it is the same and how it might be different."

Victor expected a rebuff, but instead, Darvell said, "I thought as much. I could see it in your eyes. But such things are forbidden by both churches." Victor's "I understand" was preempted by Darvell's "So we must take great care not to be caught. There was a burial today. The ground will not settle for another few days. Tomorrow night at midnight, the Ingolstadt graveyard. I will bring the shovels, together we will do the digging. A bottle of brandy with a touch of valerian will do for the night watchman."

The next night, Victor left his rooms and made his way to the cemetery. He was excited, and scared. What if they were caught? Darvell would be dismissed. He would be expelled, sent home in disgrace to face his father's disappointment. That is, if the authorities did not jail him and the church excommunicate him. Then he would be shunned with no decent person having anything to do with him.

Or maybe the rumors were true, that once he was in the graveyard he would be attacked by Darvell who would then drink his blood and use his body in other unnatural ways. Victor shuddered at this thought and was disturbed to feel a tingle of excitement run through his body along with the chill of fear. Thoughts of his friend Henry ran through his mind just as physical urges affected his body.

But Victor's lust for knowledge quickly outweighed his fear, apprehension, and the other emotions he would not admit even to himself. He continued on and soon in the pale light from the remaining sliver of the moon he found the graveyard. It did not take long until he saw the figure of his professor standing by a just filled grave marked with a crude wooden cross on which was printed the name "Anna Felder." Darvell was leaning on a shovel. Victor gave a start when he saw that someone else was with the professor. It was Fritz, Darvell's giant of an assistant.

"Ah, welcome, young Victor. Fritz here and I had a wager as to whether you would show. Some do not, their fear and caution overcoming them. But you are here, which means that Fritz's salary is not doubled this month and tonight he must do all the digging."

Darvell then threw his shovel at the large man who, with a grunt, began exhuming the corpse.

It took but an hour's work until Fritz's shovel struck the coffin. Then came the sound of splintering wood as the large man used the blade of the shovel to force the lid.

"Just the body, Fritz. Hand it here, then close the lid. Victor, take the feet. Good. Now give Fritz a hand up. Careful, don't fall in. It's where we are all bound but do not hurry your arrival. Good. Now, Victor, begin filling in the grave while Fritz and I carry this to the cart."

With the now empty grave again filled, the three left the cemetery in the one-horse cart that had brought Darvell and Fritz there. Victor rode upfront with Darvell with Fritz leading the way with a lantern. To Victor's surprise, the professor turned the cart away from Ingolstadt and into the woods.

"There's an old shed," he explained, "deep in the forest. I use it for occasions like this that require privacy. It would not do to successfully rob a grave only to be found carrying a body, well, a dead body, into one's apartment. We can work there in quiet for as long as is needed."

"And what of," Victor glanced toward the back of the cart, "that is, what happens to … the body when we have finished?"

"Fritz will carry deeper into the woods where nature, the insects, and the animals will finish most of it." He looked at Victor. "It's too much of a risk to put it back." At the young man's nod, Darvell added, "I can only imagine what might happen when the grave is opened to transfer the bones to the charnel house and they discover it is empty. There will no doubt be more talk of the undead and whoever it is in the back will become the stuff of stories with which to scare children into sleeping. All, here we are."

The shed was well hidden. Victor had not seen it until Fritz walked up to it. He suspected than even in the daytime the shed would be hard to find unless one knew where it was. It was larger than Victor had expected with two beds for sleeping, a small table on which to take meals and a large one on which to work.

Fritz carried the body in and laid it on the large table. When he unwrapped its shroud, Victor exclaimed, "It's a woman."

Victor had seen the female body before, illustrations in certain books and drawings his father did not know he had found, but this was the first time the young man had seen a naked woman in the flesh. He could not take his eyes off it, of her. Her breasts were large, now sagging in death but still fascinating, there was hair under her arms and on her legs and a mass of it between them. Despite the smell of decay, he felt himself growing aroused and this both disgusted and excited him.

"It *was* a woman." Darvell's words cut into Victor's reverie. "Now *it* is our subject. Let's get some sleep. Tomorrow we will begin, with me shaving and cutting and you taking notes. Fritz, make sure the shutters are tightly closed and we will see you tomorrow night. We should be done then."

They lay in their clothes, the room lit by only a few candles. Just as Victor was falling asleep Darvell said, "It is exciting, is it not."

Feigning sleep, Victor did not dare answer.

27

9

From the journal of Victor Frankenstein

The examination of the ~~woman~~ subject that M. Darvell and I performed may have been the step I need to begin putting everything together. We spent the entire day dissecting and exploring ~~her~~ its body. We began with dorsal and ventral examinations, with Darvell shaving the pubic hair so that the intimate parts may be examined. Once we finished with our observations of the exterior of the subject, which we had covered in his lectures although not quite so thoroughly, Darvell produced a scalpel and directed me to make the first cut. When I reminded him that I was to take notes, he replied that the only way to learn was to get one's hands bloody. And so for the first time, I cut into a human body.

After that, it was much the same as in the lecture dissections. There is nothing in the human body that is not in one of the lower animals. There are the same veins, arteries, muscles, and organs as there are in a rabbit, a dog, or a pig.

"You see, Victor, he told me, that nature is one with itself. Man himself is an animal like any other." Here he cut out the ~~woman's~~ subject's heart and held it up. "This is not the seat of love or the soul as some believed. It is a pump and nothing more, designed to move the blood through the body."

He then shaved ~~her~~ its head and, using a saw, cut off the top of the skull and removed the brain.

"Behold, Victor, the seat of our knowledge. It is what is contained in here that separates us from the lower beasts. In ways yet to be discovered, it controls our movements, gives us speech, and most importantly, allows us to think and makes us what we are." He placed the brain back into its cradle of bone.

"You will note, Victor, as we proceed, as you trace the vessels that deliver blood, as you follow the path of food from into the mouth and out of the anus, as we remove each organ and test the muscles, there is nothing that could be considered a soul, or the repository of one. So where might it be, this soul, or does it exist at all?"

I did not know how to respond to this question. Clearly, it was not one to be asked in class. Such a question would lead to charges of heresy, dismissal, and probably worse. There is a stake in a small square near the west end of the town. It has not been used since my arrival but the charring on it tells me that it has been used. I answered as best I could.

"If as you say, Monsieur, that it is the brain that makes us who we are, and we are made in the image of the Lord, then it is likely that that is where the soul resides, going to judgment when the brain stops working."

Darvell nodded. "A good answer, better than those who say it is one of the ineffable mysteries of God and who are we to question Him. And now, a consideration for later. You mention that the brain stops, as indeed it does. But when? How long after the heart stops beating and the lungs stop breathing does the brain continue to function? Do the eyes still see, do the ears still hear, does the brain still think. Alas, there is only one way to find out, and by then it is too late. But come, pick up the scalpel and let us examines the arms and the legs."

Time inside the shed did not exist, closed as it was to the outside and lit only by candles and lanterns. We worked on the subject all day and into late evening. We became lost in our work, so much so that I was startled when the door opened. At first, I thought that the authorities had found us out but quickly realized that it was only Fritz.

Again I marveled at the size of Darvell's assistant. He was the largest man I had ever seen. Judging from my own height, he must have been close to seven-foot tall. But despite his size, his face was that of a child's. He had long, flowing black hair and when he smiled displayed a full set of pearly white teeth. If one saw him in silhouette one might think him a monster, but by lantern light he was more of a gentle giant.

Darvell said something to Fritz in what I took to be their native language. Fritz responded, the first time I had heard him speak. Then he assisted Darvell and me in wrapping ~~her~~ the remains in the shroud in which it had been buried, after which the giant picked up the bundle and carried it deep into the woods.

After that, we cleaned ourselves and our workplace, dined on the meal Fritz had brought, and made our way back into Ingolstadt unnoticed.

10

From the journal of Victor Frankenstein

I have found it. Knowing that there was nothing special about the human body was the key. With this knowledge, I reviewed the notes I had made from my reading of the ancients. Agrippa's incantations were not magic, I realized, but instructions on how to make certain potions. Paracelsus wrote of substances that would poison the human body and of the curatives to be taken to prevent or cure these poisoning. But his papers include antidotes for which there are no poisons. Newton studied these writings and concluded that they were a pathway to an elixir that would prolong life and possibly restore it. The "Calculus of Creation" he called it. But having found the path he could not walk it to its end. For all his genius, he did not have the science that we have today. And once this new science was accepted, the alchemical paths trod by Newton and his fellows were abandoned as leading nowhere. But all roads must lead somewhere, and I believe that I have found the destination that Newton sought – the elixir of life. If this be so, then no longer need a son, a mother, or a wife cry out over the body of a loved one "Bring them back." We will not need the Lord, for we will have usurped His power.

11

For the next few months after his epiphany, Victor was not seen outside his rooms except for lectures and church services. And soon not even then. Professors Krempe and Waldman at first worried about him. They had witnessed the mania that could befall a student in pursuit of his education, losing himself to everything but his studies. And Victor had always been a solitary young man. Even when he socialized with his fellows, he seemed merely with them rather than of them. And they feared he may have been unduly influenced by his studies with Augustus Darvell. That had happened before, students lost due to a morbid fascination with death, one of whom decided to perform an unauthorized autopsy. The problem with that was his subject was a friend who had slept over in his quarters and was not yet dead. The whole affair was handled quietly and, under the deceit of a religious prohibition, Darvell's class no longer included autopsies, at least, officially. There were rumors, of course, but rumors are not proof.

Summoned to M. Kempe's office, Victor assured both his mentors of his conditions.

"Forgive me, Sirs, but I have taken on independent research and studies, which, when complete, will bring great credit to this university."

"And to you, no doubt."

Victor shook his head. "In some small part, perhaps. But most of the credit will belong to those who set my feet upon the correct path and urged me to make the journey. And I thank you both for that. But I have gone as far as you can take me and so I finish the journey alone."

Looking at each other, the men nodded then Waldman said, "Victor, yours is one of the finest minds we two have encountered. It was an honor to guide you. Do what you must, but try to get out some, and report your progress to us, shall we say, every few months or so. Does that sound right, Kempe?"

Kempe agreed and so Victor was left alone.

By this time he had worked out the correct formulae for the potions that would comprise the elixir. When he prepared them and mixed them, they came together to form a solution almost the color of blood but less viscous than that life-giving substance.

The first step is complete, he wrote in his journal. *Now to bring life the dead.*

But it was not to be. From the same supplier that M. Darvell used to obtain his lab subjects, Victor obtained mice, rats, squirrels, and hares. One by one he killed them by chemical suffocation, then injected them with his elixir. They remained dead. Again, he injected them and then killed them. They did not return from wherever deceased animals go.

Two and a half years, he wrote. *Time lost, time wasted. Were Kempe and Waldman correct all along? Were the ancient theories "exploded systems?" Or have I missed a step. I must review my notes again.*

Review he did, over and over then a few times more for good measure. Just when it felt that despair would overwhelm his soul, he found it. His missing step had been there all along in his notations on M. Darvell's first lecture, when the man had spoken of "the spark of life."

Was that spark, Victor asked in his journal, *that which our Lord used to bring life to His creations. Not the Breath of God but the Fire from His fingertips?*

Victor had seen reproductions of the work Michelangelo had done in the Sistine Chapel. He had viewed the artist's rendition of The Creation of Adam. Unbidden, his mind added to that masterpiece lightning going from God's finger into Adam's, to bring the lump of clay to life.

Galvani, von Kleist, and van Musschanbroek. They are the key. I must obtain Leyden jars and create a battery such as Franklin described.

Two anxious weeks passed as Victor obtained and built his equipment. Another week of testing. Then it was time. When he ran the current through his so far inert elixir, the solution darkened and thickened and became as blood.

With a breath he did not know he was holding, Victor killed a rat, let it cool, and confirmed its death as M. Darvell taught him by placing a tube against the creature's chest and listening for the silence. Not detecting a heartbeat, he injected it with the elixir.

A minute went by, and then another, and then another. No results. But then, after a few more minutes, the rat's chest moved as its small heart began to beat and its lungs took in air.

At first, Victor was overjoyed, but then tumbled back into dismay when the rat did not awaken. It was both alive and dead and for a moment the young man despaired. How should he proceed? Then, he made a decision that was a mixture of desperation and inspiration. Shaving fur off the rat's head, he drilled small holes in its skull. Placing the electrodes of the Franklin battery into the holes, he sent current directly into its brain.

One minute – breathing, no movement. Another minute, the same. More current. The third, fourth and fifth minutes, the same. Then, movement. The tiny body began to rock back and forth then shuddered. Victor raced to pick it up then placed it in its cage, just in time for it to gain its feet, squeal in protest at its treatment, then run around as if it has never crossed past the veil of death, a veil he had pulled back to allow for the rodent to do the impossible – return.

The rat – it is alive!

12

A week after Victor left for Ingolstadt, Henry Clerval visited Elizabeth. It was, as he explained to her uncle, merely one friend calling on another, to fulfill a promise he had made to Victor and he was not one to break a promise.

Alphonse was not convinced of Henry's intentions. The lord of House Frankenstein had plans for his son and his niece. No one was good enough for his family save family, even if Elizabeth's true familial was unknown. He did not need or want another suitor to interfere in the future of House Frankenstein. The Clervals, although of merchant stock, were newly wealthy and with that comes the need for status. What better way to gain that than to marry into it?

Without his wife's counsel, Alphonse decided to approach Elizabeth directly. When he did, she laughed.

"There is no cause for concern, Uncle Alphonse. Henry is a friend, nothing more. In fact, Henry is a confirmed bachelor."

Alphonse thought he knew what his niece meant, but still asked, "You mean …"

"I mean that he is unlikely to marry except for appearances' sake. And should that occur, any children would most likely be adopted."

"I understand," and Alphonse did. There were such men in his circle. He had no use for them but he let them be and as long as they were discrete, as did the law and the Church.

"Henry will be a perfect escort for me while Victor is away and will also keep the scions of the other families from daring to press their suits."

Alphonse did not approve of the young man. He did not like how the merchant class dared to claim the status equal to that of the well-born. He did not like the young man for what he was and the godless acts he no doubt performed with others of his kind. But he had to admit to himself that Clerval could be useful, a usefulness that would end once his son returned. *After all*, he thought, *it will not do for the heir to the House to be seen as close to such an unnatural creature.*

"That it will," Alphonse conceded to his niece. "Very well, then. The young man will be welcomed in this house."

"Thank you, Uncle."

Henry and Elizabeth became close friends, telling each other the secrets of their hearts. One evening, the two were sitting in the garden. It was a warm day and they were sipping cooled drinks.

"One day Victor will be home, and we will be wed," Elizabeth said this as a matter of fact and without great enthusiasm.

"Is that what you wish?"

"It is my fate, Henry," she replied, her head bowed and eyes downcast, as if weighed down by her acceptance of the inevitable path others had decided for her life. "My destiny to become Lady Frankenstein."

"You are that now," he observed.

"Yes, but I wish to be mistress of the House Frankenstein in truth and not by default. It is my right."

This last confused Henry. Elizabeth was an adopted orphaned. What rights might she have? But he forbore to ask. Instead,

"Do you love him?"

There was no need for her to ask of whom Henry asked. "I love him more than a cousin, and slightly less than a brother. I suppose that after we've married, once we have become … intimate … I will love him as a wife should her husband and then soon as a mother loves the father of her children. But if you are speaking of love as in the romances you give me to read, then no. I doubt if I ever will feel that kind of love." This last was stated with such sadness that it looked like her head would bow so much that her chin would rest upon her breast. Before Henry could reply, Elizabeth turned the question back on him.

"Do *you* love him?"

Henry's smile was wistful as he allowed words he had never before dared speak escape from his lips, "As a friend, as a brother, as … something more, yes to all. But unlike you, I do feel 'that kind' of love, one that is doomed to be unrequited. But I will always be his friend and do whatever I can to assure his safety and happiness, as I am sure you will as well."

Henry said this last in a voice that caused Elizabeth to wonder if it was a veiled threat. No, more likely it was just a man's concern for the one he loved.

"But enough talk of love and other nonsense, Elizabeth. I have Victor's latest letter. It says that he is now working alone and making great progress, although he fails to say on what exactly he is working."

13

By the time his letter had reached his friend, Victor had killed and revived rats, hares, two terriers, and a cat that he had lured into his chambers with a saucer of milk. He had learned that the larger the animal, the more electricity was needed to bring it back from the darkness.

I could not bring back the pig, he told his journal. *I preserved it, the elixir once charged is always effective. Its heart beats, its lungs breathe, once or twice it grunted as if it was going to awaken, but it did not. The spark needed is too great. Should I ever dare to bring back a man I fear I will need the power of the heavens to help me cure the death of a person.*

Victor next experimented on the limits of revival. He found that unless decomposition was too advanced, his elixir would repair all damage. He broke limbs both ante and post mortem. Again the damage was repaired. He even dared to amputate his subjects' legs then clumsily sew then back on. Although the scars from his rough sutures remained; the bones, the blood vessels, and the nerves soon knitted themselves back together.

There seemed to be no limits save that of time. That was the factor, the further away death, the longer it took for revival and recovery. And when the death was the furthest, when the animal did revive it was as if newly born, unable to care for itself.

The cat, Victor wrote, *has been killed several times now and each time it revived. No additional elixir was needed, just electricity sent into its brain. However, on the trial in which it lay for four days dead, the cat awoke confused, its mind like a new kitten rather than the full-grown cat it had been. It made a loud mew then bolted out the window before I could stop it. I cannot help but wonder what will become of it.*

I must prepare my notes for my presentation to M. Darvell. He will understand what I have accomplished and it is with his help that I will convince the others of my great victory over death itself. But first, I must destroy the remaining subjects. Decapitate them and burn their bodies lest a lighting flash bring them back.

14

About the time Henry and Elizabeth were discussing love and Victor was busy reviving dead animals, a young couple seeking a quiet place in the woods to be alone made a horrible find. Phillipe was looking for a smooth place to lay his blanket as Susanne, his *amour*, walked around looking at the flowers. When she bent down to pluck one, her eyes found the remains of what had once been a young woman. Her shrieks brought Phillipe to her side. When he saw the reason for her distress, he fought down the nausea that threatened to embarrass him in front of the girl and led her away from the site.

"That poor woman," she said. "We must tell someone."

Phillipe knew that she was right, but he realized that he would have to explain, to Susanne's father at least, why they had been that deep into the woods. Susanne quickly discerned the reason for his hesitation, saying, "Be brave, my heart. I will handle my father. He suspects anyway and now he will have no reason to refuse when you ask him for my hand." (This presented another problem for Phillipe, since despite his vows to Susanne, he had had no real intention to ask for her hand.) "Now then, we must return to the village. Be sure to mark the trail so you can lead the way back."

Two hours later, men from the village were standing in a half-circle looking down at the body of the young girl, except for Susanne's father who spent most of the time glaring at his future son-in-law.

"Does anyone know who she might be?" asked Herr Tanner, one of Ingolstadt's burgomasters. It was to him whom Phillipe and Susanne had reported their find.

"It is hard, sir," said one of the other men who had come out. "The animals have been at her and she appears to have been here for some time."

"Has anyone gone missing?" asked a second man.

The burgomaster shook his head. "No one has been reported. Possibly a stranger who wandered into our woods. Some misadventure befell her and here she is." It was the safest conclusion. No one would miss a stranger and that would be the end of it. "We will call in a priest to say a quick mass for her soul and bury her in the churchyard. Poor woman."

As one the men bent their heads and said quiet prayers for her soul. But during this reflection, talk of burial caused Peter Felder to take a closer look at the remains.

"Wait," he said, "the torn material around her. I recognize it. It looks like…" he knelt for a closer look. Unmindful of the body fluids that had leaked on to it and dried, Peter picked up a piece of the cloth. "It is, this is part of the shroud in which we wrapped my cousin Anna before we … buried her."

Despite the warmth of the evening, a chill ran through the men standing around the body.

"She was buried, was she not?" asked one.

"Yes," Peter answered, "I was there when they closed the lid. I helped carry her coffin to the grave."

"I see her clothes," said a second man, "but they do not appear to have been on her body."

"Gentlemen," Burgomaster Tanner said. "These are dark waters which we are about to enter. You four, take the blankets we have brought and wrap her as carefully and respectfully as you can. Take her to the church from where Anna Felder was buried. Peter, come with me. You other two, come with me and Peter. We are going to the churchyard. Before this night is done we must dig up her grave. And let us pray that we find her there."

Arriving at the churchyard, Tanner awakened Father Kennel and explained what had to be done.

"It is a serious thing," the priest said, "to disturb the dead."

"It is more serious," countered Tanner, "if the dead has already been disturbed and we do nothing."

After Father Kennel prayed over the grave, there followed two hours of hard digging by lantern and candlelight. The soil had compacted and both pick and shovel were needed. Finally, the coffin was exposed.

"The lid is still on," said one of the diggers. "Shall I remove it?"

"Do so," said the priest, "and let us pray that Anna is still at rest."

A lantern was handed down. The digger pried open the lid and removed it and found the coffin empty.

The man standing in the grave quickly jumped out as the rest of those present blessed themselves and made signs against evil. "There is evil afoot," Burgomaster Tanner exclaimed.

"If there is," Father Kennel said, "it does not come from Anna. Just two days before her death I heard her confession. Now none of us are without sin, and while I cannot tell you what her sins were, I can assure you that none of them would have led to the corruption of her soul and the rising of her body. Indeed, right after she died, I administered to her the sacrament of the dead, anointing her according to the prescribed rights. The Burgomaster is correct in that there is evil abroad, but the evil was not done by her. Rather, someone did evil to her."

"We will find him," Herr Tanner promised.

"I hope so," Father Kennel said. "But in the meantime, let us return Anna's body to her grave."

"Should we not burn it or something, to be sure," suggested one of the men.

The priest shook his head. "Whoever did this, whatever purpose he had for digging her up, whatever foul things he did to her body, he was done with her. Which is why he left her." Father Kennel turned to Phillipe. "The Lord led you and Susanne to that part of the woods today, young man. First to stop you from sinning and then to discover Anna's body. For your part in this, your sins, if any, are forgiven, as are Susanne's. Go and sin no more."

"He won't sin no more," growled Susanne's father, "Not without a wedding first."

15

News of the discovery of Anna Felder's body spread quickly through the town of Ingolstadt, as did rumors of how she died, how she rose up, and what she did after her resurrection and with whom she did it. Finally, two nights after she was found, the word everyone was thinking and no one dared say was uttered in a tavern.

"Nosferatu," said Rast, a large burly man who usually had too much to drink.

"What makes you say that?" Palley wanted to know. He was much smaller but also liked his beer, as long as he could get someone else to pay for it.

Rast thought a moment then, "What else could it be? He turned into mist and dropped down into her coffin. Probably had his way with her then, then misted them both. He then took her to the woods, did unspeakable things to her, and left her remains behind."

"What sort of unspeakable things, do you think?" At his question, everyone turned toward Saxer. No one liked him very much but he always had money and he bought their tolerance by buying them beer.

Palley slapped his shoulder. "Didn't you hear him, he said it was unspeakable. That means he can't speak of it."

At this bit of wisdom, they all nodded then made Saxer buy another round for daring to ask such a question.

As the night wore on, the drinking became heavier as the tavern patrons considered the evil that might be about them.

"But who could it be?" Rast wondered aloud, not expecting an answer.

Gsell spoke up. "A few weeks ago some of those …" he tried to think of an appropriate insult but failed, "…students from the University were in here, talking loud and making like they were better than us." He found his insult. "Bastards."

Everyone nodded their agreement and he went on.

"One of them, I think his name was Gaffner, said something about one of the professors. His name was …"

"It sounded like… devil," suggested a man named Elmer. "No, Duvall."

"No, not Duvall," Gsell said after a minute's thought. "It was

Darvell. This Gaffner said that this man only went out at night, that sunlight burned him, and that he knows all about death."

To most of the men in the bar that was proof enough, but Saxer added more.

"I know the man. Walks about at night when no decent man is about. I've even seen him going into and coming from the woods. A giant was with him, a long-haired beast."

And that was all the evidence they needed. As one they left the tavern in search of the evil that walked among them. Had it been almost any other night, they would have searched in vain, but on that night, Augustus Darvell had been in the woods. He and Fritz were returning from the shed when they encountered a group of drunken, angry men.

"That's him," cried Gsell, "it has to be." Everyone else agreed and charged the pair.

"Run," Fritz said in his native tongue then put himself between his master and the crowd. The large man was strong, but so were some of the others. And they had armed themselves with knives, clubs, and rocks. The mob split, some of them attacking Fritz while the others pursued Darvell.

Fritz fought as best he could but was soon overcome by numbers. He was stabbed and beaten with clubs and rocks. Soon he was unconscious but the maddened crowd did not stop. By the time his killers finished, his face had been slashed and his head, left arm, and right leg had nearly been severed.

Darvell tried to run, but some of his pursuers were faster, catching him at the edge of the woods. They beat him into submission and as he lay helpless but conscious on the ground, Rast said, "There is only one way to deal with the likes of him."

A strong tree branch was found and sharpened. Strong arms grabbed his limbs and held them apart. Then, with a rock for a hammer, Rast drove the stake through his heart and pinned him to the ground.

When dawn came, its sun shone on several men staring blankly at their night's work. They had killed and mutilated two men and were now not as certain as they were the night before of the men's guilt. The bodies were covered, the authorities were called, and the university officials notified. A meeting was held in the office of Burgomaster Tanner.

The university had sent two representatives, M. Clovis and M. Audrey. Father Kennel was there, as was Gsell. His fate, it was agreed, might be the fate of all. There was no one present to speak for M. Darvell or for Fritz.

"Well, gentlemen, how is this to be resolved? We cannot have town versus university, not again."

"We were just …"

"Be quiet, Gsell. We know what you and your crowd did. It is for your betters to decide what to do next."

Both M. Clovis and M. Audrey knew the truth about Darvell's nocturnal activities and how he obtained subjects for his nighttime autopsies. However, it had been impressed upon them that it would be best for the university if no one else found out. There was only one thing to do. After all, Darvell was a foreigner, with no ties to the country. He would not be missed. And there were those who were not comfortable with the lessons he taught.

"While we do not know the full extent of Augustus Darvell's activities," said M. Audrey, "we can state that the university had no direct knowledge of them. However, in the interests of peace of harmony among us all, we will concede that it is likely that he and his assistant did exhume Anna Felder's body and took it away, whether for experimental purposes …"

"Unauthorized experimental purposes," added M. Clovis.

"… unauthorized experimental purposes," agreed Audrey, "or for other reasons. Since her body was quite properly reburied, we'll never know for sure. Either way, the university, without admitting guilt, is prepared to make small remunerations to both her family and to the church. And that will settle the matter."

All present nodded in agreement, except for Clovis.

"Except for one thing," he said. "It can be argued that while Darvell and his assistant deserved death for their actions, it should have administered by the proper authorities. As it was, they were struck down in the street." Here Clovis looked at Father Kennel. "Struck down without the chance to confess their sins and make their peace with God. They may have deserved death, but not damnation."

"What do you suggest?" asked Herr Tanner.

Clovis looked at Gsell. "Who drove the stake into Darvell?"

The townsman shook his head. "I cannot say."

"Gsell," barked Tanner, "it was either you or someone else. If you cannot say then it was you."

Gsell thought for a moment. He knew it had been Rast. He liked the man, but he liked himself better. "Rast," he said quietly.

"We'll settle for his death. The rest Father Kennel can deal with."

All nodded agreement but there was one more bit of business. "Since it is likely that the two men died in mortal sin, it would not be proper to bury them in sacred ground," Father Kennel proclaimed.

Both Clovis and Audrey shrugged. "You can take the bodies straight to the charnel house for all we care," said Audrey.

16

From the journal of Victor Frankenstein

I learned this morning that M. Darvell is dead, killed by a rabid mob over the death of Anna Felder. His death is partly my fault. Had ~~he~~ we not stolen her body, he and Fritz would be alive. Fortunately for me, they were killed by the mob before they could give my name as their accomplice.

But that matters not for I am ruined, my last few years wasted on a discovery I cannot reveal. Yes, I have learned to bring back the dead, but it will be clear that my knowledge came from forbidden readings and practices. I will be shunned, my name and person anathema, my family in disgrace. I may even suffer the fate of M. Darvell and Fritz, my mutilated body consigned to the charnel house.

I cannot go on. Best I destroy my notes and tell Professors Krempe and Waldman that my research came to nothing. I will then withdraw from the university and return home to be my father's son.

But no, I cannot abandon the last two years, not knowing what I know, not after beating death and becoming its master. When our Lord walked this earth, He raised up many until finally with His Father's blessing He raised Himself up. This He did with by the Power of Heaven. I, a mere man, have duplicated his feat. I have revived the dead. Does this make me His equal? Or have I surpassed Him? I know not. I do know that since I've heard of Darvell's death my mind is in constant turmoil, fear of exposure one minute, despair the next, and pride that I have become godlike in my knowledge and ability.

But here in Ingolstadt, they would not understand. Without Darvell's support, they would call me mad if I even hinted at what is possible. They would not listen, would not be convinced even if someone were to be raised from the dead.

That is the answer. What are rats and dogs and cats – what became of that cat? – compared to the majesty of the human body. Let me bring back someone from the dead and they must listen. I will tell them that no longer will their loved ones be lost to death but rather, I can restore them and make them whole. I will keep the process to myself and make them pay. And all will be amazed at my power.

Or would I be condemned by those who come after me? Hailed for my knowledge yes, but vilified by how that knowledge was used. Kings who live forever, undead armies forever waging an unstoppable war, the world overcome by too many bodies trodding upon it. All that would be laid at my door, my brilliance ignored in favor of the vilification of my name.

I feel a mind fever coming on. I cannot proceed and yet I must. I must not be like the ancients and step off the path, not even if the path ends in death and destruction. But it shall not be those twins of despair because thanks to me there would be no death.

If He is not too jealous of what I, his mere child have accomplished may God help me. I know not what to do.

Except that I do. I have to know that if after bringing back to lower animals I can raise up God's ultimate creation. If I cannot, them all I have done is just an elaborate conjuring trick. But if so …

Those worries must come later. First, my journey must be completed. And to do so, I will need the help of M. Duvall and Fritz one last time.

17

It was fortunate for Victor that no one cared or gave much thought about what happened to those bones and bodies consigned to the charnel house. It was a place most people prefer to forget existed, for it was a reminder of their inevitable fate and final journey. Neither a temporary grave nor family crypt matters much to time and insects.

By day, Victor concocted copious amounts of the Elixir of Life. Based on his experiments, he knew the approximate amount that should revive a human. There was a bit more calculation to work out how much charge would be required to create the spark of life. He ran the numbers again and again. There did not exist a known battery large enough to do so. That would have been the end of his plan had he not recalled the storm he had witnessed when still at home. Surely lightning from heaven itself would be more than sufficient. As for the method of calling it down, that took only the barest thought and the simplest logic. Like many buildings in Ingolstadt, his was protected from the storm by a Franklin rod. The large metal pole somehow attracted the lightning and guided it by cable into the ground below. As chance, or maybe Fate would have it, this cable ran outside Victor's window. When the time came it would be an easy matter to redirect the fury of the storm.

Still, he needed a body. It was only at night that he dared visit the charnel house. The need to know for certain overcame his worry about getting caught stealing the dead, which might cause his role in the Anna Felder case being revealed. Several times he almost resigned himself to take the path of safety and final ignorance, but he knew that too long a delay would render Darvell's body useless to him. So reaching down into his passion for victory and greatness, Victor fought off growing doubt and persistent pain in his head as if they were demons tempting him to surrender his soul. In the dark of the first night of the new moon, armed with a bullseye lantern, he searched the charnel house for the remains of Darvell and Fritz.

Elation banished both doubt and pain when he found them but then dismayed. Darvell's body was ruined, the stake driven through his body having ruined his heart. But Fritz's body was more or less intact save for his head, arm, and leg.

But Victor knew, or at least prayed, that the elixir would repair such damage if the wounds were stitched up, however roughly his fingers worked the needle and thread.

In fact, Victor had pinned his hopes on this being the case. With no one to help him – it was not as though he could hire a seamstress to assist his endeavor – he completed the job the murders had begun and severed the large man's body into more manageable pieces. He let the flesh drain of blood then wrapped each piece. Lastly, he removed Darvell's head and wrapped it carefully, almost tenderly. Victor held more emotion for the pieces of the giant than he had for the man himself. He carried his parcels back to the cart and rode back to his apartments.

The night's work was not yet done. Under cover of the remaining darkness, he carried each piece up to his rooms. There, he roughly sewed Fritz's body back together and with a bone saw removed the top of his skull. Fritz's brain wound up in a bucket to be replaced with that of M. Darvell. He then sewed the calvaria, what a lesser intellect might call a skullcap back on before injecting the composite body with half of the Elixir of Life he had prepared.

18

From the journal of Victor Frankenstein

It has been two hours since I injected what I can only call my creature with the elixir. Thus far, there are no signs of life. I have given it more elixir, hoping that it would help. I can only hope that it is working in a way that is not yet externally discernable.

Two more hours and the body of the creature is changing. The sutures appear to be healing, although it is obvious that what scars there are will remain. The skin is becoming yellow as if jaundiced. The lips are black as coal. In all, it is a horrible sight and not at all what I expected. I shudder to consider if it might be better if the elixir does not work. I hate myself for the doubt but that does nothing to lessen it.

It is now early evening and I am weary from lack of sleep, last night's toil, and the fear of being found out and brought to a similar end as my fellow conspirators. I yearn to close my eyes but dare not. There would be no one to bring me back.

Night has fallen. As I observe my creature by lantern light, I perceive the faint rising and falling of its chest. I place a tube to its chest, yes, there is breathing and the heart is beating.

It is alive and yet not. Preserved now from further decomposition as the elixir will continue to heal it. Now I need only a storm.

19

The storm came a week later. As the sky darkened and the clouds rolled in, as thunder crashed in the distance, Victor took the cable he had spliced into the one that ran from the Franklin rod into the ground and attached it to several conductive bolts he had drilled into the creature's shaved head. He had at first thought to attach them to its neck but discarded this idea in favor of direct electrical stimulation of the brain. Fearing that Darvell's brain had been in his dead body too long, and remembering what had happened with the cat, Victor had secured Fritz's body with the strongest leather straps he could find.

The storm came closer. Victor counted the time from seeing the distant flash and hearing the thunder. Three miles away. Soon, the light and the crash came quicker – two miles. One mile. Then the storm was upon him.

Lightning lit the sky as the thunder boomed all around him. Victor prayed for one strike. One meager, life-giving bolt was not too much to ask from one creator to another. He worried –were the connections tight, what if a fire started, would there be power enough to raise the dead?

All at once the building shook as power was already racing down the cable. The body on the table convulsed as its back arched. The leather straps strained but did not break and the air filled with the oddly pleasant – at least to Victor – odor of seared flesh.

Apparently, one strike had been too little to ask as the Creator answered his prayer many times over. Another strike, and then another, and then another, Fritz's body dancing violently to Heaven's tune. Victor wanted to approach it but was afraid to touch the creature for fear of feeling the lightning himself.

So he waited. Waited until the storm had passed before approaching the body. Had the power of the storm given true life or had it stolen what the elixir had given? Victor checked the straps, then removed the wires running from the main cable. Only then did he have the courage to examine his subject.

Yes, it was breathing. Yes, its heart still beat. Both were stronger, more rapid. But its eyes remained shut and there was no other movement.

I have failed, Victor thought and began to consider what he would do with the body. Was it worth the risk of returning to the charnal house? Before he could form a plan, from the corner of his eye Victor saw something more beautiful that anything he had witnessed in his life thus far. The hand lifted from the table. It was but a slight movement, but movement nevertheless. There followed a low moaning from its throat. And as Victor stared with all his being, its eyes opened wide and stared into the face of its new creator.

It lives. I have given life where there was death. I have become like God!

But as he looked down on what he had wrought, as the newborn creature greeted him with a savage moan instead of speaking, as it struggled against its bonds, Victor saw his creation for what it was.

It was not as Victor imagined. It was not beautiful, it was not Augustus Darvell resurrected. Instead, its skin was horribly scarred where he had sewed its limbs and stitched its wounds. The wounds on the animals had been hidden by fur. This creature's body was mostly blue and purple, pale green, with patches of yellow and brown. Its staring watery eyes were blank, with no intelligence behind them. And the sound it made. It was the noise of a wounded animal unable to understand why it had been hurt. It was the wail of a dog beaten by the master it loved and not knowing why. It was the cry of a soul in distress, one suffering the agonies of Hell despite not having sinned.

The lightning had sparked life, but it was not human life. And when the man who in his mind had become God looked upon his work, he did so in despair and did not find it good as had the One he imagined himself equal to. Instead, he abandoned his creation, running from his room and into the street of the town.

The creature watched Victor escape, his newborn mind swirling in wordless despair, unable to imagine what sin had he committed to make his creator flee from the sight of him.

20

The evening sky was clear after the storm, the air filled with the lingering smell and ozone taste left behind by the lightning. There was a distant rainbow, an apparition which caused scientists to argue about its cause even as others marveled at its beauty and remembered God's promise. In a tavern in which some days ago anger over a young woman's disinterment led to three deaths, the man called Saxer said that should one find the rainbow's end, all one's troubles would be solved.

"That's only if you're a Celt," Gsell countered, "but I suppose that that would solve most of your problems."

"But not all of them."

The argument may have gone on most of the night, the men in the tavern using it to forget that less than a week ago they had murdered two men and that one of their number had died for what they did. But then,

"Excuse me."

Everyone turned to look at the stranger who had walked in. He was young and his youth and his dress told the men that he was a student. The fact that he had come into this tavern so soon after the recent tragic events told them that he was new to town.

Maybe a month or two later, they might have cuffed him and thrown him into the street, but just then they had no taste for violence of any kind. So Saxer simply glared and in a rough tone said,

"What is it?"

The stranger gave the address of Victor Frankenstein's lodgings and asked, "Can someone direct me?"

"A round for the house will get you what you want," said the barman.

The young man had long ago learned the art of getting along and the value of exchange. So he smiled and said, "Why not?" Drinks were ordered and poured and paid for and the young man left armed with directions to a location that was not that far away.

As he turned onto the street he sought, he was amazed to see his quarry running toward him. Catching him in his arms, he cried out, "Victor, my friend, good to see you after all these years."

Victor looked at the man who had embraced him. In the

confusion of his mind, he just stared, and then for just a moment, his troubles faded.

"Henry, my friend and brother. What are you doing here? You should be at home, in Geneva."

"I am home, Victor, for the next few years. My father plans to expand his business to the Levant and the countries east of it. Because of that, he needs someone who can speak the languages. As so, he had finally consented to send me to the university where I will be studying Persian, Arabic, and Hebrew. And possibly Sanskrit. But wait, you seem quite upset as if running from the devil himself. What is the problem?"

"You have stated it, Henry. It is the devil himself, and that devil may be me."

"A bit hard to run away from one's self."

"You have no idea. I have done something both wondrous and awful. I have committed the sin of Adam and dared to eat from a forbidden tree. I fear I have created an abomination."

"Surely, my friend, you exaggerate. It cannot be that bad."

"You think so? Well, it may be even worse. Even thinking about it makes me shudder at what I almost unleashed upon the world. Come, come up to my rooms and you will see. And maybe you can tell me what I must do."

Willing but confused and worried, Henry Clerval followed Victor to his lodgings. This was not the reunion for which he had hoped. But his friend, his brother by choice, and his secret love was in distress and he hoped he could relieve him of his mind's burden.

When they got to Victor's apartment he led Henry to the backroom, the room where he had brought the dead to life, the room where he had his creation strapped down. But as they entered the room, all the two men saw was an empty table with broken straps, and a broken window.

"May God forgive me," Victor exclaimed in anguish before collapsing on the floor, "the monster is loose on the world."

21

He remembered it all. As his life spilled out of him, Augustus Darvell remembered it all – his recognition of the woman who was his mother, his first awareness of himself and the world, the terrors and joys of childhood, his first kiss, his first love, his first heartache.

School – first in the village and taught by a man who had been a priest but was one no longer. Then at the university in Wallachia. His meeting with Fritz and the start of a lifetime relationship, more a friendship than master and servant. The trip west, to Ingolstadt and his teaching post.

As always, good and bad times. His fascination with death, which was natural given his homeland. His students, few of whom understood what he was trying to teach them. A good life, until the end.

The end. At the end was Victor, his most promising student, who in the end told him that he knew how to change the world and needed his help. The finding of the body, the hurried clean-up, the attack by the villagers.

Had Victor betrayed him? Traded his life for his teacher's and Fritz. Fritz's sacrifice. "Run," his friend had cried and he had run but in vain. He remembered being brought to the ground, his limbs held fast, the stake piercing his heart.

He remembered dying.

The brain does not stop at death. The electrical impulses that give true life sustains what is called the self, the spirit, the soul of the person. But not forever, that would be cruel. Without the heart, the lungs, and the blood, the spark of life slowly fades, taking away all that makes up the individual. The past is recalled then forgotten. And so Augustus Darvell first remembered then lost his mother, his childhood, his loves, and his heartaches. He lost everything save the memory of his death, the sharp stake taking his life. And as this last moment of life faded, so did his awareness of that life, and when that was gone, so was Augustus Darvell.

First, there was the fading light, then darkness. For a long time that was all there was. The heart pumping, the lungs breathing, the blood flowing, but there was nothing to the creature that lay upon the table. The body lived but there was no soul, no spirit, no spark.

Then there was pain, pain that convulsed the body, pain from the power that surged through it. Each time the lightning struck there was more and more pain, and this pain would be the first memory of the one on the table.

It hurts, the being thought, not yet knowing who or what it was. He cried out at the pain, his first words. Slowly, his mind began to awaken. It was the mind of an animal, all instinct and hunger and fear and need. He felt himself tied down and struggled against his bonds, bonds designed to secure even the strongest man. But the being that was held by these bonds was not a man and might never be. The elixir that pumped through his veins along with his renewed blood made him stronger, as had the repeated lightning strikes. He strained against the leather. They weakened, then snapped.

Free, was his second thought, the word coming unbidden. As mind became to recognize thought, he climbed off the table then fell as his legs betrayed him with ignorance of their purpose. The creature struggled as his mind and body sought to remember how to move. He rose up again, his awakened brain somehow now recalled how to stand, how to walk, how to run.

Flee. He looked around but there was no place to go. He was barely able to see beyond a blur. Then the light from the window shone into his pupils. The brightness triggered a response that needed no direction from the brain. His eyes focused, adjusted, and saw the outside.

Instinct caused him to grab covering to protect himself as he crashed through the window, unmindful of the glass and uninjured by the fall. He ran down dark and empty streets until his legs carried him out of town and towards the shelter of the woods. There was something in the woods, something that had not been forgotten when the mind of Augustus Darvell ceased to be. So the creature, who was still more animal than man, more instinct than mind, ran for the only shelter he knew and did not stop running until he came to a mostly unknown shed that lay deep in the forest. There the creature collapsed and, exhausted, fell into darkness, unsure if he would return but too weary to care.

The creature woke into the light of the morning, alert the way an animal is alert, lying still, sensing the air around him – its scent, its tastes, its sounds. There was nothing that frightened him, no signs of danger. So he moved. He was hungry, sore, and confused. Thoughts he did not recognize and could not process worried his mind, but they were put aside in favor of more immediate needs. He stood and looked around. Had he been the either of the men from whom he had been made, he would have seen books and journals, plates and cups, and the tools of the scientist. But he was not those men so nothing was familiar. He knew only that his body was sore and his stomach was empty so he staggered into the daylight in search of food.

Berries and roots were his breakfast, and water from a stream quenched his thirst. He walked around, exploring its territory, looking for threats.

Twigs snapped and leaves crunched. The creature was able to hear the intrusion long before the ears he had in his first life would have been able to. Three men were nearby. Instinctively he paused, lay down, and was still. They walked the other way, away from him, away from his shelter. Growing animal cunning told him to flee deeper into the forest, but something else drew him back to the shed.

Every day after that was the same as the first, going naked into the woods, foraging for food, fearing and avoiding those who walked in it, and returning to the shed at night to sleep.

Slowly though, as days became weeks and the weeks month, his brain began to remember, thoughts returning to synapses that were healed enough to fire again. The mind that had been Augustus Darvell was gone, but the brain still held much of what he had learned. He began to recognize chairs and tables, beds, and books. He remembered their names and what they were for. He opened some of the books, but the words were a jumble so he closed them. Likewise the journals, the ones on a table and the one he found in the robe he had carried away with him when he made his escape. He knew it was writing but what it said was a puzzle to him.

Most of all, he knew himself to have been a man, and set out to become one again.

22

*F*rom the journal of …

It has only been a few days since … I have come to be me. Whoever I am. That I do not know. Nor do I know how long I have been living in this shed, or how I came to be here. Maybe the books will tell me. I can read them now.

Whoever I was must have been an educated man, for reading and writing comes easy to me. Here in this shed are works such as Plutarch's Lives, and The Sorrows of Werter, and Paradise Lost. I feel I know them but do not remember them. I care not for the first two but the last, the fall of Satan, somehow calls to me.

It is the journals in which I am most interested. Whoever wrote them, and I feel that it may have been me, used this place for work he wished to keep hidden. He cut open animals and men to study and learn of them. Why, I ask myself, did he need this knowledge? To what benefit is it to know how blood flows or how the lungs breathe. Maybe the man I once was, if indeed I was that man, could answer. Maybe that answer will be found in another journal. There are still many to read.

I may have to leave this place. More and more men come into the woods and it is all I can do to avoid them. I fear that if they find me, I will hurt them or they me. I have been testing the limits of my body and find that despite the large size of my body, which does not feel natural to me, I am quite agile. I am also very strong. A large dog attacked me in the woods the other day, it was chasing a cat before it turned on me, and I caught the beast around the neck as it leapt at my throat. One squeeze and it was no more. Being hungry I tasted its flesh. It did not please me and I think I will stay with roots, berries, and other gifts of the forest.

The cat had scars similar to mine, so very alike that they could have been stitched by the same hand. The cat stopped once I ended the dog and rubbed itself around my legs. It was the first time I can remember being touched by another living being.

I found it pleasant.

Later, a man came in search of the dog, letting out a loud cry when he found it. It was a cry of loss and anguish, and soon other men had joined him. From my hiding place, I heard them speak of a creature who haunts these woods. They called it beast and monster and said that it must be hunted down and destroyed. It was only later that I realized that they were speaking of me, that I was the monster.

Yes, it is time to leave. I will take my robe, what useful tools there are, the unread journals, this book in which I write my thoughts, and the other books besides. I will go deeper into the woods and either find or make a shelter. For if found, I will fight back rather than be taken or harmed, and in doing so I may become the monster they think I am.

23

Deep in the woods, an impoverished family lived on private land. The father, M. Emile De Lacey, was of noble birth and had once been wealthy. But he had fallen on hard times. Politics, along with poor choices and investments, served to ruin him, and with ruin came bad health that caused him to be blind. It was only through the kindness of the owner of the land, a M. Jacques Defreyne, that they any had shelter. Defreyne had been a friend of the man, one of the few who stood by him during and after his troubles. While he could not openly support his friend, either politically or financially, he did allow him and his family to stay on his land. There was room to grow food, a nearby stream provided water, and the animals of the woods provided meat. It was not a luxurious life, but they had food, shelter, and love.

By day, the man's son Felix hunted and did what needed to be done to maintain their small cabin. His sister Agatha and his wife Safie tended the garden and took care of the old man. At night, after their evening meal, they would discuss their day then take turns reading from the books De Lacey had brought with him or playing and singing songs on a guitar. In all, they were, if not happy, at least content with their lot.

"Our mystery benefactor was here last night," Felix told the family one night during dinner.

De lacey turned his head toward his son. "What did he leave this time?"

"Two rabbits for the pot and wood for the fire."

"Where do you think he comes from, and why does he do what he does?" Safie asked, not for the first time, for the benefactor had been leaving such gifts for some time now. The previous Fall he had begun leaving firewood and come winter he had cleared away the snow from around their cabin. It was only in the spring that he had been leaving small animals.

"It is sometimes best not to question these things," De Lacey replied. "He does these things for his own reasons, and should we seek him out, he may move on. No, leave him be, Felix. Should he want us to know him, well, he knows where we are."

"I would like to meet him," Agatha said, "if only to thank him."

"I have heard that there are spirits in the woods, some good, some evil, like fairies and ogres, and monsters."

"That's it, wife," Felix said with a smile, "no more reading of Perrault for you. Next you'll be seeing a red-caped young girl being chased by a *loup-garou* while searching for her grandmother." They all laughed then De Lacey felt for and found his guitar and began to sing:

"Stay on the path, my darling, and do not stray.

For there are beasts out there who would take you away.

Beware of false promises and beware of false men

Stay on the path for it leads the right way."

And they sang and laughed until the candle flickered. Only then did they turn in, unaware that on that night, as on many nights before, someone listened at their window and wished that he could be part of their family.

24

It was the music that first drew Victor Frankenstein's creation to the De Lacey's lonely cabin. He had taken refuge in a cave, one with a small stream that ran in the back and a natural chimney that allowed the sun to shine down into it. He felt it safe, since the outside was covered by dense foliage making it difficult for passersby to see it. He had only found it by accident. There were men hunting him. Men from whom he had stolen clothing and food. He thought them asleep but one had heard him. He fled as that one roused the camp. With torches and lanterns they chased him through the night. He had good night vision and was able to elude them but they were persistent. By chance, he found the cave's entrance when he hid behind the bushes that concealed it. They passed him by. That was good, since he did not know what he would have done had they found him.

No, he knew and wished he didn't. He would have fought them and possibly killed them. He had no wish to be a monster.

But it could be that he was. He had seen his reflection in the water, when he peered into the still waters of a pond and ugliness looked back. His mind knew what beauty was and it was not a scarred head and ravaged features. He pulled away from the pond and had not looked into one since.

It was his second night in the cave and he was considering staying there for a time. It was clean and there was food enough to be found outside it. It was a safe haven and would give him someplace to read the remaining journals and again contemplate the struggle between Satan and his Maker.

Then came music, not that the creature knew what music was. He had read of it but had never heard it. And when he heard the guitar, when he heard voices joining together in song, the soul that he did not yet know he had yearned to listen to it and so he followed the sound. It was not long before he found the cabin. He sat outside it and marveled at the wonderous noise from within. And when the music stopped, the family talked, and he wished he could have joined in. Were he to dare try, how would they react? Even to his ears, his voice was harsh and grating. He suspected it may have been from lack of speaking. He had no one to speak to and perhaps his voice was horse from disuse. Or perhaps his voice was as horrible to behold as his face.

Night after night he listened to the family play, sing, and talk. By day he watched them, taking care not to be seen. He learned their names and their relationships and they became a tremendous part of his small world.

When he saw that the one called Felix had to go deeper and deeper into the woods to find wood for the fire, he began gathering it up and at night leaving it by the cabin. *In exchange for the music,* he told himself but he knew that it was also his way of taking care of people who had become dear to him. And when he was not at the cabin, or gathering and eating food, he would talk to himself, reading aloud from his books and, as he had hoped, gradually his voice became less harsh, less grating.

It was, for him, an idyllic situation. He was safe, at peace, and, save for certain urges he felt when he saw the two women, had no wants or desires.

But things change, as they always must. He grew careless and was briefly glimpsed once or twice. The De Lacey family became aware of him and talked about him but at least they did not seek him. All was still well, until he read the last journal but one.

It smaller than the rest and he had found it in the pocket of the robe he had with him with when he first became aware. It was in a different hand, which at first he had trouble making out. When he did, he read of the deaths of the men called Darvell and Fritz and the theft of their bodies. He read of the joining of brain and body and of an elixir that gave this joining a kind of life. And he read of the lighting drawn from the sky to awaken the creature on the table. And he read of how the creature's maker had in horror rejected it.

I have created a monster were the last of the hastily scribbled words.

Had there been anyone in the woods that night near the cave, they would have heard the cry of a soul in anguish. Pitiful wails that came from the one inside the cave as for the first time tears rolled down his cheeks. It was he of whom the journal wrote. It was he whom his creator had abandoned and called a monster.

He cried through the night, resisting the urge to lay about him and destroy everything in sight. He almost did, but with his last bit of reason he knew that what little was there was all he had. So he collapsed on the bedding he had made from leaves and the stolen clothing that had not fit him and cried himself to sleep.

The next morning he did not feel better but he had a sense of calm that had been unobtainable during the previous evening of tears. The painful knowledge of his creation did not change his circumstances, at least that was what he told himself even knowing that was a lie.

Taking up one of the pencils he had carried away with him from the shed, he made an entry into his own journal.

I have learned of my own birth and how I came to be. I was made from the body of one man and the brain of another. I was cut apart and sewn together. Like Adam, I am a new creation and live in a kind of paradise. Like Satan, I have been cast out by my creator who deems me not worthy of love or even existence. And I know things my creator does not, that while the mind does not last after death the knowledge that was in its brain is somewhat retained. And I know my creator's name. On the first page of his journal is written the name "Frankenstein."

25

It was late spring. Agatha, Felix, and Safie had gone into town to meet with M. Defreyne who managed what funds the family had left. At his insistence, M. De Lacey remained behind.

"You do not need an old, blind man slowing you down. Enjoy yourselves. M. Defreyne has a large house. Large enough for some needed privacy I would think, Felix, Safie. And Agatha, there should be some young men about. It is past time you met some. No, go, it is only for a few days. There's plenty of food and it is warm enough that I will not need a fire."

In truth, De Lacey would have liked to accompany them, to meet and talk with his old friend again, the only man he could trust, the man he had to trust for if Defreyne betrayed him all would be ruined. But the old man had a reason for remaining behind.

That night, after his evening meal, De Lacey sat quietly in his cabin, waiting and listening. Finally,

"You can come in, my friend. The rest are gone."

He heard first the door open, then heavy footsteps come in.

"You knew I was out there," said a hesitant voice, one that had never before spoken to anyone.

"I hear you most every night. My hearing is very good. Now then, find a chair and sit down. How are you called?"

A long pause. If De Lacey had not heard his visitor's breathing he would have thought himself alone. Then,

"I have no name. I was abandoned by my creator when he made me."

"God abandons no one."

"I am sure of that, but He was not my creator. Have you time to listen to my story?"

"All night and into the day. And there is food and drink for when we need it."

The creature told his tale. And when he was done, the old man could do nothing but shake his head.

"Terrible, terrible,' he said, both in pity for the creature and anger as his treatment. Then he asked, "So which are you, Adam or Lucifer?"

"I am both, Sir, and neither. If I must be called something, call me by my creator's name, 'Frankenstein.'"

"I have heard of that name. There is a House Frankenstein in Geneva. Its master was Alphonse. Who rules it now I know not. But know this, M. Frankenstein, you are welcome in this house at any time, even after my children return."

Thank you, Monsieur, but … I do not know. Your blindness does not let you see what I am. I am a monster of a man, if I am a man at all. My face is hideously scarred and those few who have seen it have either attacked me or run from me. I would not frighten your family."

De Lacey snorted. "If my family rejects you because of appearance than I have failed both them and you. But I do not think that will be the case. Now then, they will not be returning for a few days. Let us make the most of them and spend our time telling stories and singing songs."

And so they did, Frankenstein returning to his cave during the day and spending his evenings with De Lacey, who sang him songs and told him stories and taught him of the good and evil of other men.

"If I have counted my days correctly, they will return tomorrow," De Lacey said one evening. "Wait a day after their return, then come after sunset. I will hear you. I will tell them about you. They already know of your kindness. I will warn them of your appearance. Then I will invite you in. And I pray to God they will receive you as I have."

Felix, Safie, and Agatha did return the next evening. Once settled, Felix related all that had happened between him and Defreyne.

"He is still your good friend, Father, and he missed your visit. But he has been a good shepherd to your finances, so there is no need to worry on that account."

"Yet, Felix, your voice says that is something about which to worry."

"M. Defreyne is not well. He tells me that he has only a few years left. But he has hopes that with the changing political situation, he can arrange for our safe return. But if his health gets worse …"

"It is all in God's hands, my children. But now I have news. I have met our benefactor. I heard him the night you left and invited him inside."

There were cries of protest from his children about how he might have come to harm from inviting a stranger inside. "And yet I am still here. His seems to be a kind and gentle soul, although one that is also tortured. He calls himself Frankenstein and I believe him to be of that house. He is, however, like us, an outcast, having been rejected by his … father. He will be here tomorrow night and I will tell you this, he is a large man whose face is horribly marked. I have felt his scars. Do not judge him by his appearance but rather by his manner. Now then, it is late and we must all rest."

That evening De Lacey slept soundly. His children did not. M. Defreyne was sicker than Felix had let his father believe and the son worried for the futures of himself, his wife, and his sister. Then there was this stranger, this benefactor who had suddenly revealed himself. What did he want? Who was he really? And what designs did he have on them?

Safie also worried. She had known poverty before Felix had saved her. She did not care to return to it. She suspected that Defreyne had been kindly lying to Felix, that there was no money, that their purchases had been made not from their account but by him. Should he die, they would have nothing.

Agatha was excited. Like her father, she chose to put the future in God's hands. She worried about the present, the present where no man she had met in town looked at her in the way a man should look at a woman. Maybe this stranger, despite his appearance, would look at her that way.

The next evening, with his family gathered after dinner, De Lacey waited until he heard his new friend outside.

"Come in, M. Frankenstein, and be welcomed."

Again he heard the door open and heavy footsteps come in. Then he heard cries and gasps and a scream from Agatha and was ashamed of his family.

A hoarse voice said, "Forgive me, I will go and not bother you again."

Before De Lacey could object, Agatha called out.

"No, Monsieur, it is you who should forgive us. Father tried to prepare us but your appearance, even by candlelight it is quite startling. Please, as my father asked, join us."

"Yes, please," echoed Safie.

Felix also invited Frankenstein to stay, and he, pretending not to see the young man put down the axe he had instinctively grabbed, accepted.

That night there were few songs sung and no stories told. Frankenstein excused himself saying, "If you will permit, I will return tomorrow evening."

"Come during the day," Agatha said. "I would see you as you are in the light, for it by the light of day that our fears are dispelled."

"Yes, I would like that," the creature said.

26

From the journal of "Frankenstein"

It has been several weeks since I revealed myself to the family De Lacey. They are becoming used to my appearance. The lady Safie has stopped turning away from me and stares at me sideways. The lady Agatha looks at me directly. M. De Lacey tells me what he knows of the outside world. Felix ignores me and, I believe, resents me. I understand. I am the outsider, and possibly he sees me as a rival for the women under his protection. Although I have done nothing improper toward either one, I must confess my body has responded to the closeness of the women, especially Agatha. But such thoughts are just that, thoughts only. In Agatha, I see the beauty that I lack, and I would in no way pollute that beauty. She needs a man to love not a … whatever I am. Thanks to the De Lacey's I no longer feel myself a monster, but I am surely not a man. There may be nothing to do but move on. M. De Lacey had told me of Geneva and how to get there. Perhaps it is time to seek out my creator and demand of him whatever it is a father should give his son. At the very least he should give me a name of my own.

27

Happiness. That was what the one who called himself Frankenstein had begun to feel. It was a new emotion to him, a feeling of contentment that ran through his body when he thought of his life. The De Laceys were an important part of that life now. He was spending more time with them than in his cave, and when M. De Lacey suggested that maybe an additional room could be built on to the cabin, no one, not even Felix objected. As for his growing feelings toward Agatha, he had decided to discuss these with her father and be guided by his advice and to accept whatever his decision was. Frankenstein no longer worried about how he came to be or why his creator had abandoned him. He thought himself more as an Adam than as a Satan for he felt he was approaching a type of paradise.

But in his happiness Frankenstein forgot that every Eden contains a serpent, and that sometimes the serpent's choice is not yours to make but is thrust upon you.

On the day the serpent came, Frankenstein awoke in his cave. He had not planned to go to the De Lacey cabin until later that day. There was bedding to replace and food and firewood to gather. He would finish his work, eat lunch, then go see what he had begun to think of as his family. Maybe that day was the day he would speak to M. De Lacey.

It was late that morning that three men rode up to the cavern. They were clearly men-at-arms and bore the crest of the House de Freyne. When Felix went to greet them they roughly pushed him aside and barged into the cabin.

"We are from M. Defreyne," their leader said, addressing De Lacey. "You are on his land and must pay him rent or leave."

"I do not understand. Defreyne is my friend and it is by his leave that we live here freely."

"You speak of Jacques Defreyne. He died last week, and now his son Étienne wants his land cleared of all beggars and intruders."

The old man raised himself from his chair and turned toward the voice of the leader. "How dare you, sir. I am Emile De Lacey and I am no beggar."

"We know who you are," said one of the other men. "Your name is a joke, the poor beggared family who lives in the woods. A man who was less important than he thought and ruined himself and his family. So pay up or be gone."

Felix had recovered quickly. When he ran into the house to defend his father he was grabbed and held fast by one of the men.

"But we have no money," De Lacey said sadly, "and nowhere to go. Please show mercy and give me time to speak to Étienne."

"Monsieur, our orders were quite specific," said the leader, "and it is unfortunate for you, for all of you, that the showing of mercy was not included. Since you can neither pay nor go, you leave us with only one option."

The leader drew his sword and ran it through the old man. On seeing their father murdered, the women screamed and Felix broke away to grab his axe. But an untrained man armed with only an axe is no match for trained soldiers with swords and to the continued screams of Safie and Agatha he quickly joined his father in death.

"What of the women?" the second man asked over the cries of the women. "They're going to die anyway."

The leader shook his head. "No, let them meet God untouched by us. Our job is killing, not defilement. Now quiet them for good."

Frankenstein was walking toward his family when he heard the screams. Dropping his load of firewood he began running. When he arrived he saw three men coming from the cabin. They were using what he recognized as Safie's and Agatha's dresses to clean their swords.

Too late, was his last thought before a red rage filled his mind. With a loud cry, he rushed forward.

The soldiers were at first startled to see a large, hideous creature running toward them. But they were well trained. They stood their ground and let the beast come to them. When he was close enough they began to slash and stab with their swords.

What had once been a man who called himself Frankenstein was too fast for the three men. Such was his rage that he did not feel what wounds he received. Instead of being laid low, he grabbed the sword arm of the first man he encountered, twisted it, and broke it. Then he did the same to the man's neck. The second man was likewise slaughtered, only when Frankenstein twisted his arm it came off. The man fell dying as his life's blood pour out of him.

The third soldier ran. Looking back he saw that the Devil himself was chasing him and that the Devil was faster. A hand on his shoulder and his collar bone was broken as he was thrown to the ground.

The chase had somewhat calmed Frankenstein's mind. No longer the mindless beast that had effortlessly killed two men, he was now something more terrible, a man avenging his family. As he stood over the fallen soldier, he asked, "Who sent you?" putting his foot on the man's chest so as to emphasize the importance of his question.

"De…Defreyne," the soldier stammered out.

"Jacques Defreyne said to do this?"

"No, he's dead. It was Étienne. He gave the order. We had no choice."

"Then neither do I."

Then the creature who had been a man when he awoke that morning, whose humanity had abandoned him when he saw his family's blood being wiped from swords, slowly pressed his foot down on the soldier's chest, breaking his ribs and stopping his heart.

He dragged the soldier's body back and threw it into the woods along with the other two killers. He took what he could use from the cabin - the books, some clothes, a cloak from the largest soldier – then removed the bodies of his family. These he buried in a clearing among the trees.

28

From the journal of Frankenstein.
My family is dead and all is lost. I cannot remain here. I will go to Geneva and demand an accounting of my creator. But first I must pay a visit to Étienne Defreyne. It was his order that killed my family. It was by his order that I was once again cast out of Paradise, and it will be by my hand that he dies. Tonight I am neither Adam nor Lucifer. I am instead Michael, God's avenging angel.

29

The house of Étienne Defreyne was well guarded, his bedroom on the first floor, overlooking the garden. It was once his father's but now it, along with everything else the old man had owned, was his. Life for Étienne was good and as he placed his head on his pillow he was content.

As he slept, Étienne did not know that a large man who had eluded the guards of his estate was just below his window. With his dark cloak hiding him from the night, the man, if such he was, climbed the balcony outside his window, the same balcony from which Étienne had viewed his garden.

Despite his size, the man moved silently. No one, not the guards below or the sleeping man within, heard him enter the bedroom. Étienne had no idea that the man was even there until he felt his bed move and two hands around his neck.

Étienne woke up but the pressure on his throat kept him from crying out and the man's weight kept him from moving.

"Emile De Lacey," came a whisper in the dark. "Felix De Lacey, Safie De Lacey, Agatha De Lacey. Do you know these names?"

The look in Étienne's eyes told the man that he did.

"Good, remember them as you burn in Hell."

The man started squeezing, going slowly so that his victim would feel it as his life left his body. Étienne thrashed but soon fell still.

His family avenged, the man left as quietly as he came. As he left the Defreyne estate, he whispered, "And now, to Geneva."

30

Victor Frankenstein's illness lasted four months. It started with fever and delirium, with Victor suffering through fever dreams and muttering about monsters and God. It was unclear from his words if he was God, the monster, neither, or both. Henry stayed with him through the long months, leaving only to attend lectures and class. Nothing he or the nurses he hired could do relieved his friend's suffering.

What had caused it? Henry wondered. What had brought his friend so low? He thought of their meeting in the streets of Ingolstadt. Victor's nervous excitement, his talk of "the sin of Adam" and having created an "abomination." And what of this monster Victor was supposed to have loosed on the world?

Something had escaped from the workroom. And Victor was in no condition to explain what or who it might be. "I hope it wasn't a who," Henry said one day to a cat that seemed to be always about. In desperation, he turned to Victor's journals, thinking that somewhere in them there would be a clue as to what had caused his friend's condition.

He began his reading in mid-afternoon, following Victor's course of study. Much of it was beyond his knowledge and he had no interest in philosophers either old or new. Then he came to Victor's association with M. Darvell – the study of the dead, the robbing of the grave, the illicit autopsy.

By then it was night. Henry continued reading by the light of a candle. He read of Victor's breakthrough, his discovery of the elixir of life, and how he tried to use it to revive dead animals. With a growing chill that had nothing to do with the temperature in the room, he learned of Victor's discovery of lightning as life's spark. *That*, he thought, *explains the strange apparatus in the back room.*

The journal entries stopped with Victor's decision to try to revive his teacher.

"Victor, my dear friend," he asked the suffering man on the bed, "what have you done and why did you do it?"

He pictured it in his mind – the lighting, the revival, the madness of what Victor had called monster and abomination. *Thankfully, it broke free and escaped.* Henry thought as he looked out the window and toward the now starlit woods. *It must have died, or else there would have been reports of such a beast. Or maybe there were? I have been too busy tending to Victor, or attending class, or … seeing to other needs. Talk of beasts and monsters is bettered suited to taverns than classrooms. But it does not matter. Dead or alive, captured or killed, the important thing is that it cannot be traced to Victor. No, the important thing is for Victor to get well. But how?*

It was morning of the next day. Henry had fallen asleep in his chair, Victor's last journal open on his lap. A thought had occurred to him just before he dozed off. He stood and found the journal in which Victor had recorded his making of the elixir. His notes were very detailed.

I could do this. But dare I?

He looked at his friend, moaning in the clutches of another fever dream.

He is dying. I have no choice.

It took him most of the day to prepare the elixir according to Victor's recipe. It took him a good part of the evening before he found the nerve to use it.

"Forgive me, my friend. However this turns out, forgive me."

Slowly pushing the plunger of the syringe, he injected his friend with the hopefully life-saving elixir.

31

Slowly, Victor Frankenstein opened his eyes. A crack at first, his lids barely lifted as he allowed light to come in. Then he opened them wider, seeing nothing but the ceiling. He knew where he was, in his own apartment, but did not remember anything past coming back with Henry and finding the monster gone.

The monster!

Victor bolted upright and almost passed out at his sudden rise. Strong arms wrapped around him.

"Easy, Victor, easy. You are safe and well." He knew the voice. "Now lie back down."

"Henry, my friend. How long?"

"Were you out? Four months. But know you are back with us. Thank the Lord it worked."

"Four months? It seems like only yesterday. Wait, what worked?"

"Know this, Victor, your life was despaired of. Physicians, surgeons, the finest minds in Ingolstadt all examined you and all they could tell me was to keep you comfortable until the end. I could not. You are as a brother to me and I would not abandon you to death." Henry pointed to the table on which he had stacked Victor's journals. "I read them, Victor, read them all and I know what you did, and how you did it."

Again Victor rose from the bed. Grabbing Henry's arm he cried, "For God's sake, Henry, please tell me that you did not bring me back from Death's gate!"

"Be easy, my friend, I did not. You had not crossed that way, although I think you were in sight of them. I prepared the elixir according to your very detailed instructions and injected you while you still lived."

It took a moment for Victor to realize what his friend had done for him. Then, "Thank you for that, Henry. For if I had died unconfessed, I would surely have been condemned for my sins. What of the monster?"

"Dead, or gone. There have been no reports of him."

"That is good."

"And now that you're whole again, you can write up your discovery of a medical elixir that cures, well, probably everything."

Visions of the fame he had sought ran through the recovering man's mind. Then he remembered the animals on which he had experimented.

"No, that must remain between us. I did not test the Elixir of Life on living creatures, only dead ones. Should its secret become known, it may be that anyone treated with it will never know death. Or if they do die, they would not decay as they should. No, I will concentrate now on the comparison between alchemy and science, and how the former might instruct the latter."

Victor and Henry stayed two more years at Ingolstadt, both finishing their studies at the same time. Victor's thesis was well-received, although it was not the groundbreaking paper for which Messrs. Kempe and Waldman had hoped. It won no prizes but was deemed acceptable for a degree. After receiving less than enthusiastic congratulations from his teachers, Victor wrote to his family to tell them of his impending return after several years away.

It was two weeks before they left, two weeks during which they journeyed through the countryside. They slept in the open, enjoying God's nature. On the last night before their return, as they each lay in their own bedroll, Victor asked,

"Henry, are you still attracted to your own kind?"

"If you are asking if I seek physical comfort with men, yes, I do. There are quiet places in Ingolstadt where men who are likewise inclined gather."

"What of the authorities? If they should learn of these places ..."

"They know and do nothing, as some of those in authority frequent them. And what of you, are you still faithful to Elizabeth?"

"I am, and our marriage is one thing I look forward to on my return home. I only hope ..."

"Rest easy, my friend, I believe that she has been as faithful to you as you were to her."

"And if she has not been?"

"Then on your wedding night pretend not to notice. We all have secrets, do we not, my friend."

"Yes, Henry, we do, although some are darker than others."

The next day they set out for Ingolstadt. On their arrival, Victor found a letter waiting for him at his rooms.

32

*M*y dear Victor,

We received with joy your letter telling us of your return home. However, it pains that I must respond to your letter with one of sadness. Your brother William, that sweet, gentle child whose smiles delighted us all and warmed our hearts, is dead, murdered.

Four of us went for a walk – myself, Elizabeth, and your two brothers went to walk in Plainpalais. When it grew close to dark Elizabeth and I sought William and Ernest but they were not to be found. We rested on a seat and waited for them. Soon Ernest returned alone. He said that William had run away to hide himself as he sometimes did but that he could not find him.

William and I sought him while Elizabeth waited should he return. When night fell, we returned to the house in the hope that your youngest brother had returned. Alas, it was a vain hope and so I roused the men of the house and, armed with torches, all of us searched through the night. It was not until the church bells tolled Lauds that I found him.

My cries of anguish caused the others to rush to me and it was then they beheld the terrible sight. My son, my lovely child who had not yet seen seven years of age, was stretched out on the grass. He was livid and motionless, the marks of his killer's fingers clear on his neck.

In sad procession we conveyed your brother home where there was nearly another tragedy. On seeing the corpse of her cousin, Elizabeth cried out, "Oh you darling child. I have murdered you." Then she fainted.

I knew that it was not she who murdered the boy, for she had been with me the entire afternoon, and at the house after that. For a time it appeared that Elizabeth would be lost to us as well, but with great difficulty we revived her. On her recovery, she stated that at his request, she had lent William a valuable miniature of your mother. This was not found on his body nor anywhere around it, and it is thought that it was for this that William was murdered.

Victor, please return home without any delay. Elizabeth is distraught and blaming herself. Only you can comfort her and us. But come without thoughts of vengeance against the monster who slew your brother. Come with feelings of peace that will heal House Frankenstein. When you enter this house of mourning, do so with kindness and affection, and not with hatred for your enemies.

> *Your affectionate and afflicted father,*
> *Alphonse*

33

Hiring the fastest coach available, Victor and Henry returned to Geneva. They were mostly silent on the way back home. What was supposed to have been a celebratory return was now a mournful duty.

"Had I been there, Henry, I could have saved him," he told his friend. "When my mother died, I demanded the Lord to bring her back. My cries went unanswered and so my studies led me to do what He would not, to bring back those we love. Had we not gone on holiday I could have revived my brother that morning, and let the others proclaim it a miracle of God."

"You could yet, Victor. We have some bottles of the elixir and the means to make more."

Victor shook his head. "No, my friend. It is a good thought but too much time has passed. I could revive poor William's body but his mind and spirit have left his body. All I would succeed in doing is turning the body of my sweet brother into another monster."

"My God!" Victor exclaimed suddenly, almost standing up in the coach. "It is my fault! I have killed my brother."

"That is not possible, my friend. You were nowhere near Geneva when your brother was killed."

"Read my father's words. He called the one who killed William a monster and rightly so. Anyone who would slay a child must be one. Think, you read all my journals save the last, for that was in the pocket of the robe that my creature stole when he fled my rooms. He may have learned to read it and from that discovered my name. The name of his creator, the name he came to curse. He has come to Geneva to wreak vengeance on me by destroying my family."

"Victor, calm down. You are overwrought. What you say is not likely. Think not as a grieving brother but as the scientist you are. Where is the proof? Proof that the creature is still alive. Proof that it is more than a mindless beast. Proof that it retained your journal and learned how to read it. Proof that it was able to learn where your family dwells."

Victor calmed a little. "Perhaps you are right, Henry. But as with faith, sometimes one needs no proof to be certain of something. But I will put aside my suspicions for now. But mark me, if my fears come to be founded, I will devote my life to destroying that foul beast, even if it costs me all I have."

There was silence again until they neared Geneva, both men with their own thoughts. Henry was glad that he had not been present when the boy was killed. All too often, men like himself were unjustly accused of terrible crimes just because of who they were, or rather, whom they loved. Victor spent his time reading and rereading the letter from his father, trying to find meaning and cause in it. He dwelt on father's last lines and tried to find feelings of peace, kindness, and affection but his mind kept straying to thoughts of vengeance against the monster who killed his brother, a monster he feared he created.

Their carriage slowed as it approached the gates of Geneva. There was heavy traffic both entering and leaving the city. There was nothing for the two men to do but look out the window and watch the people and horses go by.

"Henry!" Victor cried, pointing out the window. "There, in the distance, do you see him?"

"See who, Victor?"

"It is him, the monster, the one walking away, the large man with the black hair. He is the image of Fritz, into whose body I placed Darvell's brain." Victor paled and dropped back into his seat.

"I see many people, Victor, and one, I will grant you, is a very large, very ugly man. But that does not mean he is your creature. The Lord, in His wisdom, made many ugly people and that poor soul may just be one of them."

"But the scars, I saw the scars."

34

From the journal of Victor Frankenstein

"Many men have scars, my friend," was what Henry said to me when the one I believed to be my creation passed near our carriage. He said that it was my grief that caused me to believe that. I pray it is so. I had thought to tell the authorities that the one I saw was known to me, that I had seen him in Ingolstadt and knew him to be a violent man.

"The authorities are not stupid, Victor. They will find this man, as large and ugly as he is, how could they not. If he is unknown to them, they will send for someone to come from Ingolstadt to identify him. If he is recognized as the revived body of this Fritz, then you, my friend, will have many questions to answer, and those answers may lead to your condemnation. But should our friend be naturally ugly and a stranger in town, your word may be enough to hang him, whether he is innocent or not. No, I suggest that you leave the discovery of your brother's killer to the law and God. Or else you might be lost."

There was wisdom in Henry's words. So I resolved to remain silent. And now I fear that should my suspicions prove correct, my sins against God and man will come to light and my father will lose another son. Against this happening, I will leave word for Henry on what to do should I be hanged, and trust that the elixir that flows through my veins needs only the spark of life to revive me.

35

Victor's arrival home was one of joy and sadness; joy that he had returned to the bosom of his family and the sadness caused by his brother's death.

After being dropped off by Henry, who was anxious to see his own family, Victor was greeted first by Ernest. "Welcome home, brother. Come in and rest yourself in your own home. I have sent the servants for my father, who is still trying to console our cousin. Poor Elizabeth, she still blames herself for Williams's death. And Father is sinking under the weight of his misfortune. It is as if House Frankenstein labors under a curse, but for what sin I do not know."

Victor did. Even as he sat at a table with his brother, he knew in his heart that his was the sin. He had dared to be as God and for this sin of Pride his family had been cast from Paradise. Silently he prayed that whatever curse had befallen his family would rest solely on him. It was not to be.

His father came in. A small smile briefly lit up the old man's face when he beheld his oldest son. Victor stood and embraced his father.

"Victor, is it good that you are home. Would that you had never left for then maybe this dark cloud would not have rested over our family. But these misfortunes are not your fault. Nor is your brother's death and Elizabeth's agony the whole of our troubles. Tell him, Ernest, for I cannot."

"I was hoping you could have one night at home before the full weight of our house's misfortune fell on you, brother, but there has been an arrest in our brother's death."

"But that is good, is it not. What manner of man would do such of thing?"

Inwardly Victor thought he knew the answer. The manner of man that he himself had created. He prayed many prayers in the moment between his questions and his brother's answer. That it was not his creature, or if it were, that the creature would be mindless, or at least, had no memory of how he came to be. He also prayed that the journal the creature had escaped with would be lost.

"Sit and I will tell you, for it is news that should not be heard while standing. I am much afraid that it was no man at all who did the deed," Ernest said. *Then I am lost*, was Victor's thought. But then his brother continued.

"It was a woman, or rather, a girl who Inspector Keller says committed this foul act. Worse yet, it brings more anguish upon our house, for it is our own Justine Moritz who is being held for this crime."

"I cannot believe it. Justine was the kindest of creatures. She cared for our mother when she died. And it was to her that our mother entrusted the care of William. Why would she do such a thing, if indeed she did it? What evidence is there against her?"

"Justine took ill the day after our brother's death. She was confined to her bed for several days. During this interval, one of the servants went through her clothing and found the miniature of our mother, the one that William had with him when he died, the one said to have been the reason for his murder. The servant told another of her discovery and the two, without consulting any of the family, went to a magistrate. They have since been dismissed for their precipitate action but the damage was done. Magistrate Keller ordered her taken into custody. When she could not or would not account for her actions or whereabouts on the day of William's death he arrested her."

"But, Ernest, there must be some mistake. Surely no one in the family thinks her guilty."

"Elizabeth does not, which only adds to our cousin's despair. I, I do not know."

Alphonse spoke up. "I do," he said. "The girl who we took in and trusted as if she were part of the family has betrayed that trust. That such depravity and ingratitude could have existed under our roof sickens me and the sooner she leaves this world the better. Maybe then we can start to heal."

"And what does Justine have to say, how has she defended herself?"

Ernest shook his head. "Not well. She says only that on hearing of William's disappearance she went out on her own to search for him, but she told no one about this. She says that she returned too late and that the gates were locked so she spent the night in a barn. The next morning when she returned and saw William's body she took to her bed."

"I am surprised that William's body did not rise up and accuse her," Alphonse growled. "and love her or not, for I believe that we all did, there is no doubt as to her guilt, for she confessed."

"To Magistrate Keller?"

"No, to the Reverend Gerber."

"But Justine was Catholic, why not confess to a priest?"

"There was none available, and so she confessed to the Calvinist."

"And he betrayed her trust."

"He did, brother, saying that it was for the greater good for he feared that if he had not, an innocent might be blamed."

If I am right, an innocent was blamed, and might hang, Victor thought. *I should tell all, but to what cost? My words would only bring more sorrow to my house.*

"She, of course, denies ever having confessed to causing William's death. She says that she had committed sins, who among has not, but not that of murder."

"Her life is in God's hands now," Alphonse said. "She is to be tried tomorrow. If she is innocent, he will move the jury to acquit her. If she is guilty, she will be hung and then her soul will be in His hands."

The trial was quick and by all reports a fair one. The evidence was laid out against her. Despite an eloquent defense during which she denied all the charges and an impassioned plea from Elizabeth who rose from her sickbed to defend her favored servant, the jury voted for her guilt and the magistrate condemned her.

36

"Justine hangs tomorrow," Victor told Henry when they met at the Clerval home the night of the trial.

"So I heard."

"When she does, when the rope snaps and her neck breaks, it will have been me who killed her, not the hangman. I am a coward, Henry, and for my cowardice she will die."

"How so?" Henry asked, although he knew the answer.

"I should have spoken up, told the truth about the monster I created. How it escaped, came to Geneva, and killed my brother in revenge for having made and abandoned it."

Henry shook his head. He loved Victor Frankenstein as a brother but now it seemed that his friend was sliding into the deep depression that had claimed Elizabeth and was threatening to take Alphonse. The woman because she was convinced that she was partly responsible for William's murder and that the girl who was like a sister to her had been innocent of that murder. The father for another reason. He believed that Justine was guilty, and his harboring her in his house had led to his son's death. There was, he knew, only one thing that could be done, short of the impossible task of breaking Justine away from the authorities.

"It is not too late, Victor. Let us go to Magistrate Keller's home this very night. Let us tell him that despite the evidence, despite having found your mother's portrait in Justine's possession, despite her confession, and despite her unwillingness to account for her actions, the girl is innocent. Let us tell him that the true murderer is a creature with your professor's brain in his assistant's body. Let us tell him that you brought this creature back from the dead, and that, without guidance, it found its way to House Frankenstein where it knew your kin by sight and murdered one of them. Let us tell Magistrate Keller all this. And once he hears what we have to say, our families can come once a week to the madhouse to visit us."

Henry poured Victor a drink while his friend thought over what he had said.

Nodding his agreement, Victor said, "Then she and I are lost."

"Maybe not. I have an idea but before I tell it to you, let us see if there is an explanation that fits what we know. Once there is a real possibility of Justine's innocence, then we can go on."

"My friend, I believe that you already have one."

"Of course, I have, Victor. You may be the smarter of we two but I am more clever. Now drink up and I will let you in on my plans.

"Justine refuses to tell where she was on the day of William's death. Why? Either she was the killer or she was doing something else she did not want to reveal. Possibly something sinful. Now think, although we think of her as a girl, she is instead a young woman, a very attractive young woman."

"You are a poor judge of that, my friend."

"I know a beautiful woman when I see one, even if I do not desire her. Now, young women have desires the same as young men, or old men for that matter. The fact that she spent the night in a barn is telling. I hope that I do not shock you, Victor, when I tell you that I have spent a few nights on the hay in a barn with a handsome farmhand. Perhaps she found her own farmhand, or else she and her lover just used it for a private liaison."

"But why would she not tell us that?"

"Because she was a good, Catholic girl serving in a good Catholic house. Such a revelation of immorality might have caused your father to send her away."

"Knowing my father, it might have caused him to take liberties with her as he has with other of our servants."

"Another reason for her silence. As for the portrait, this is more of a guess than the first, it may be that the murderer, not wishing to get caught, planted it to place the blame on her."

"That the monster knows my house well enough to kill one of the household directly then another by stealth scares me, Henry. He is as smart as he is evil."

Having drained his glass, Victor arose to refill it. When he sat back down he asked, "So we have established that maybe Justine could not have killed William because she is as carnally inclined as you."

"Not all of us remain celebrate out of love for our cousin," Henry replied with a smile. "Let us say we have similar interests."

"Nevertheless, tomorrow she still hangs. Now, what is your idea?"

"As you say, tomorrow she hangs and will be dead. But does she have to remain dead? You brought bottles of the elixir with you from Ingolstadt. And judging from your journals you are no stranger to grave-robbing. You just need to convince your father that it would bring great comfort to Elizabeth if he allowed Justine to be interred in the family crypt. Once she's entombed, we inject her body then wait for a storm."

37

The church bells were ringing Terce when the jailer removed Justine Moritz from her cell and led her to the scaffold. They were accompanied by Magistrate Keller whose duty it was to again pronounce sentence and by Revesrend Gerber who was to offer a final chance at repentance and salvation. They were met by a crowd that had begun gathering just after Prime and a man in a black hood who waited for her at the top of thirteen steps.

Quieting the jeering and bloodthirsty crowd, Magistrate Keller read out the charges against Justine, those of abduction, robbery, and murder. He then stepped aside to allow Reverend Gerber to approach the condemned.

"Your last chance to fully confess your sins, my daughter," he said.

"I am not your daughter, and you are no father to me. If you were you would not have lied and betrayed me. I have confessed my sins and so am clean in the eyes of the Lord." To the crowd, she proclaimed, "I am innocent of the crimes to which I am accused. I know this and more importantly, my Lord God knows this. I die trusting in His justice and Mercy and I forgive Magistrate Keller, who did his duty as he saw it, and I forgive the hangman, who must do his duty as the Law demands. As I pray for salvation, I also pray for most of you to join me in Heaven." With this, she pointedly looked at Reverend Gerber and whispered, "Most, but not all. I do not think we will meet again." Then aloud, she said, "Kind sir, do your duty."

The hangman placed a black hood without eyeholes over Justine's head. He then put a rope around her neck and tightened its noose. "Go to God, my lady." He whispered then stepped back and pulled a lever. The door on which Justine had been standing fell away. Her body dropped, her neck snapped, and human justice was satisfied.

38

Earlier that morning, the family Frankenstein rose about Prime. Elizabeth wanted to attend what she called Justine's murder. Alphonse was against this, and neither Ernest nor Victor thought it a good idea but did not deny her. Victor said that he would accompany her there and comfort her afterward.

"It is my duty, as her cousin and possibly more." When he said this he looked at Elizabeth, who blushed at this first mention of their possible future. She favored Victor with a rare smile, there had been so few since William's death, then excused herself to make ready.

When she left, Victor said, "Henry has agreed to meet us there. He was a great friend to Elizabeth in my long absence and I believe that his presence will also comfort her." When his father nodded, Victor went on.

"Father, I have a great favor to ask. Allow me to claim the body of Justine and bury it in the family tomb. There need not be any service, but she was a part of the family and a great comfort to Mother."

"Who placed the care of young William into her care, and we all know how that ended. No, I cannot permit this woman to lie in the same place as the boy she killed."

Victor was prepared for this refusal. He had earlier enlisted the aid of his brother who now spoke up.

"Then why not bury her close to the family crypt? I believe it would be a comfort to Elizabeth to be able to visit Justine's grave and talk to her spirit."

"But she is a condemned murderer," Alphonse protested.

"One who had confessed her sins and stands ready to face the Lord and His judgment," Ernest argued.

"But what will people say if we allow her to lie among us."

"They will say, Father," Victor said, "that Alphonse Frankenstein is a kind and forgiving soul who after justice is carried out practices the mercy our Savior so often preached."

Alphonse was for a long moment. It was only after Victor prompted, "Do it for Elizabeth, Father, who one day will be your daughter," that he finally nodded his head.

"Very well, for Elizabeth. But do it quietly and bury her in the back of our tomb so that it is not readily visible. And no priest and only a simple marker. And mention her no more to me for as I hope to always remember William, I pray that I will forget how he came to die and who took his life."

"Thank you, Father."

Accompanied by Victor and Henry, Elizabeth watched Justine die and wept. Putting his arm around her, Victor said, "There, my dear cousin, it is almost over. Father has allowed us to bring her body home where she will lie close to the family vault."

"Thank you, Victor. That gladdens me. I think that once she is at peace I will be as well and will begin to smile again as I plan my future."

"Our future, dear Elizabeth, which I hope will not be long in coming."

They held each other close, and Victor dared to kiss her gently on the lips, to which she had no objection.

Henry cleared his throat. "If I may, we have a family member to bring home."

Leaving Elizabeth with Henry, Victor claimed Justine's body and arranged to have it transported to the family cemetery.

"What services do you wish, good sir?" asked the undertaker who had received the remains.

"Wrap her for burial, that is all. She will go into the ground as she is."

When Victor returned home he found that two ground servants with whom Justine had been friendly had already dug her grave.

"We, too, believed in her innocence and so we did her this final service," said one, a large, handsome youth about Justine's age, and Victor wondered if it had been he with whom she had spent her fateful night in the barn. *It does not matter*, he thought although if he had, the youth lacked courage for not speaking up to save her life.

Victor thanked the men and gave them coin. "No sir, it was for Justine that we did this."

"Then go to the tavern and drink to her memory and salvation."

"We will. Thank you, good sir. Shall we return later to fill in the grave?"

"No, M. Clerval and I will do that, as our last service to her." *Second to last*, he amended to himself.

"Very good, sir, and thank you again."

"We're going to do what?" asked Henry. He and Elizabeth had arrived to hear the last of Victor's conversation with the men.

"Why not have them fill it in, Cousin?"

"Because, I can't very well ask them to fill in an empty grave."

Elizabeth gasped as Henry exclaimed, "What jest is this?"

"It is very simple," Victor replied in all earnest. "I will not place one who is almost a family member in the cold ground, not when there is room in the family vault."

"But what of Uncle?" Elizabeth asked.

"What of him? He comes here only on All Saints or when there is an interment. Even then, there's poor lighting inside."

"But where shall she be lain?"

"I do not think, dear Cousin, that my great aunt Maria would mind the company, do you?"

Elizabeth then threw herself into Victor's arms and kissed him harder than he had kissed her. As their bodies pressed together Victor felt his body react to their contact. Elizabeth felt that too and asked, "Are you certain that you do not want to be married sooner rather than later."

At that moment Victor was not, but his reply was interrupted by the arrival of Justine's body. Victor thanked and rewarded the undertaker's men then he, his cousin, and his friend waited until they had departed before the two men filled Justine's grave as Elizabeth watched. At Victor's urging, she remained outside as he and Henry provided Great Aunt Maria with company.

While in the tomb, Victor asked, "Did you bring it?"

"Yes, my friend" Henry drew from his coat in which was a syringe that contained the Elixir of Life. "Are you sure this is enough?"

"It will be. She is a small girl." Taking the syringe, Victor injected its contents into the body. They did not, however, disturb Victor's great aunt. Instead, they placed Justine's in a darkened corner behind her. "We'll retrieve her tonight. There are old ruins on the ground in which we can hide her."

The deed done, Victor and Henry escorted Elizabeth back to the house then went for a walk. "Of course," Henry observed, "with Justine in the tomb and not in the ground it makes it easier to retrieve her."

"Yes, now all we need do is wait for a suitable storm and drill some holes in her head."

"No, Henry, I cannot bear to destroy her beauty in any way."

"Then what, bolts in her neck?"

"Don't be absurd. Not close enough to the brain or the spine. I was thinking that thin metal netting around her head and body would do the job nicely."

39

"What if the metal netting does not work?" Henry asked.

The storm was rolling in, it would be upon them in an hour or so. On seeing its clouds gather, Victor and Henry removed Justine from her hiding place and brought her to the ruins of an old mansion. There, in a high room that was partly open to the sky, Victor set up the Franklin rod and ran its cables to the net surrounding Justine's body.

She was unclothed when they removed her covering. *Like the last one, like Anna Felder*, Victor thought. For the second time Victor looked upon the body of a naked woman, at the curves of her hips, the fullness of her breasts, the hair between her legs that hid the treasure that most men desired. As happened the first time, the rush of desire surged through his body and soul, all of him warmed by the lust of a man for a woman. Only this was no dead woman who could be considered a mere laboratory subject. No, thanks to the elixir, Justine, although in a state of suspension, was alive. Her blood flowed, adding color to her skin. Her lungs breathed. The gentle rise and fall of her chest drawing his eyes to her moving breasts where they lingered until he tore them away, ashamed by his lustful thoughts.

Victor looked at his friend, grateful for his company. If Henry had not been there, what sin might he have committed?

In answer to Henry's question, Victor replied, "If the net fails and the storm persists, we will screw in the conductive bolts. I brought the tools with me."

"And why did you bring the axe?"

Passion fled Victor as he answered. "Should I be wrong about being able to fully restore Justine, if it becomes clear that she is going to be a monster like my first creature, I will remove her head, burn her body, and foreswear the elixir and the playing of God."

"And should you succeed?"

"I do not know, my friend, I do not know."

It was not long before the rain started and, once again, the time between the lighting and thunder grew shorter.

"She is well strapped down?"

"Yes, Victor."

"The leads are attached?"

"Yes. All is ready, Victor. She is in God's hands now."

"No." The retort was sharp with the edge of anger and arrogance. "God allowed her to die. She is in my hands."

Lightning and thunder came together, power from the sky striking the Franklin rod over and over, each strike causing the body on the table to arch and jerk. To his surprise, Victor felt the power of the storm himself, the elixir in his body responding to the spark of life falling from the sky, making him stronger. They became as one, Justine and him, and before her first moan he knew that he had given life to what had been dead.

"Quickly, Henry, let us quickly and carefully detach the leads before the lighting strikes again."

They did so and unwrapped the girl from metal netting.

There was moaning, only moaning. Victor feared to look into Justine's eyes should he see a blank, mindless stare. But he forced himself and was relieved when her eyes looked back in recognition.

"M. Frankenstein!" the young woman shouted. "Where am I?" She struggled to arise and failed. "Why am I bound? Why am I unclothed? Have I been damned and this is my punishment?"

It was Henry who threw a sheet over Justine's nude body and his voice that calmed her by saying, "Hush, Justine. M. Frankenstein and I are no devils, and this is not Hell. You are safe and we are your protectors."

"But how, why. I remember hanging, and dying. Why then am I alive?"

It was Victor who told the tale on which the two had agreed. "You seemed dead to all, even to us. But when we claimed your body I could tell that the hangman had failed his task and that there was still a breath of life left in you. I told Henry and we agreed to remain silent, lest you be hung again. We brought you here where no one would find you. I used my university training to restore the spark of life in you."

Victor motioned to Henry to unstrap her. Slowly she sat up, keeping the sheet around her for modesty.

"Did you ..." She looked down at herself then at Victor.

"No, we did not. It was necessary to fully examine you. Forgive us any liberties."

Justine blushed. "For giving me back my life I would grant you whatever liberties you requested."

Victor shook his head at her offer, again ashamed of his previous lustful feelings.

"I have clothes," Henry said and offered her a bundle. "I hope they fit."

Without shame Justine dropped her sheet and dressed, Henry and Victor turning away while she did. "What will become of me?"

"When morning comes Henry will take you to the station and a coach will take you to Lake Como." Victor handed a punch of coins. "Here is money enough to start a new life under a new name."

40

From the journal of Victor Frankenstein.

I explained my absence by saying that Henry and I were out walking and got caught in the storm. Which was, in part, the truth, even if we had sought out the storm.

She lives. Justine Moritz is alive. Today Henry saw her off with her not knowing that she may live much longer than most. I may as well, if an accident does not befall me. Now I know that although I created one monster, I can restore the newly dead, and so let one cancel the other. By this act, might my soul now be washed clean?

But this is a great power, one I must use responsibly. I only pray that I shall.

I think that I must go away. I need time alone to decide how and if I should use this power to restore the dead. What if somehow the secret comes out? I think the latter would bring ~~grave~~ *serious consequences. I can imagine the clash of two great armies. As men fall, they are brought to the rear lines where they are injected with the elixir, shocked by massive batteries, then sent off to fight again, each man suffering death after death. No, those who wage war care little for those who do their fighting. To them, bodies are counters in a great game and the dead merely one way to keep score. And there are always pawns who are either willing or forced to play.*

No, my secret if revealed will be kept by the rich and powerful. All others will die but they and their evil will live on and on. And I will then be responsible for having created monsters worse than the first one I made.

No, I must go away and think. A walking trip to Mont Blanc. And on that trip, I will consider what is to be done next.

41

From the diary of Elizabeth Levenza

Victor has abandoned me again. He says that he requires time alone, to "plan our future" he says. When I asked how he hoped to "plan our future" without me, he had no answer, just that once he returns from Mont Blanc he would then be free to concentrate on all his duties.

As if marrying me would be a duty. There was a time not so recently that I thought we would soon be wed, when I felt his manhood press against me as we embraced in the cemetery. But that may have just been lust for a woman, any woman, and not the loving desire of a man embracing the woman he wishes to marry.

So possibly Victor sees marrying me as a duty, one he owes to his family so as to continue the Frankenstein name. If so, I accept that, for it is my duty as well. Not one that I owe to my uncle but to my mother.

For as I have written before, I know the truth. My mother was no widow, left by the death of her husband to raise a child alone. No, she never married, unless one considers two bodies coming together in passion a marriage of sorts. It was from that brief coupling she shared with a passing captain of the guard that I was conceived and through that conception that she was cast out as Eve was when she sinned with Adam. Was that possibly their sin? Was the forbidden fruit their discovery of the pleasures of the flesh? How like a cruel God to deny His creations joy that came not from Him but rather each other.

But I speak of something of which I know so little. I do not know what it is to be with a man, nor with a woman, although I have had offers from certain friends along those lines. I know I should have been repulsed by such offers but was instead curious and if I was like Henry and had desire for my own kind I might have consented.

Instead, a close friend has told me of a method by which a woman can herself relieve certain physical tensions. I have tried this in the privacy of my bed and believe it will sustain me until my wedding night, and even after, if Victor proves less than an ardent lover.

When Victor returns home, we will speak of marriage. While

I do not love him with the passion I should, he may at least satisfy my desires. But more importantly, I will marry him and no other, for only by becoming the bride of Frankenstein may I reclaim the name that was taken from my mother. As for the other, if my husband does not ignite my fires and then quench them, there may be others who will.

42

"M. Clerval?"

Startled, Henry turned toward the voice that had called to him. He was not expecting to meet anyone this far into the woods. He had come from the ruins where he and Victor had secreted the elixir and the means by which it might be activated. Since the man who had addressed him knew his name, he did not feel him any threat. Had robbery or worse been a motive, he would have been struck from behind.

He turned and addressed the man, saying "Yes, how may I help you?" as he looked the man over.

He was a large man, well over six feet and close to seven. His back hair was cut shoulder length and as he smiled he displayed a full set of pearly white teeth. But for the scars on his face, he might have been handsome.

Suddenly his friend Victor's words, his description of his creation, came to him and he knew who, or rather what, he was addressing.

Terror raced through Henry and he turned to flee only to be stopped by, "If you run, I will catch you. And if I wanted your death I would have it already, and I would not leave your body where my creator could find it and bring you back as he did that girl."

"You, you were watching?"

"Yes, I have been watching my creator and his house for some time now. And yes, it was me that he saw from the coach. I did not know him then but I know him now."

"The boy, William, did you …"

"I do not kill innocents, M. Clerval. Even had I wished to, how was I to know him? On my arrival in Geneva, I knew only the name Frankenstein. It took time to learn more. I have killed, yes, but only those were deserved it."

"And does Victor Frankenstein deserve death?"

The man did not answer. Instead, he pointed towards the ruins. "Let us go there and talk. There is much I would know."

"What is your name?" Henry asked when the two were seated at the table on which Justine Moritz had so recently lain.

"I have none. My creator did not give me one before abandoning me. Call me monster, as he did the night he brought back the girl.

Call me creature. Call me Augustus. For that may have once been my name. Call me Adam or Satan. Or you could call me by my creator's name, Frankenstein. It does not matter."

"You did not answer whether you think Victor deserves death. What are your intentions toward my friend?"

"All men deserve death. It is their fate, a fate which my creator wishes to deny them. But I have no desire at present to harm him. I only wish to speak with him, to demand of him an accounting of why he brought me into this world only to cast me out. And to ask of him that which a father owes a son."

"And if he refuses?"

The creature shrugged. "I do not know. But I would ask something of you, M. Clerval, that we meet here again and you tell me of my father, and what you know of my creation."

"And should I agree but bring others, ones who would take you in custody?"

"That you would ask that tells me that you would not. But if you should, their deaths will be on your hands. I have learned that weapons might harm me but will not kill me. I still have a bullet inside me from a farmer who thought I was hurting a child I had sought to save."

Henry nodded. "We can meet here in two days, at the same time. Is there anything you need?"

The creature shook his head. "The forest provides most of my needs. As for anything else, I am large and can move heavy things. I have money from doing odd work for farmers and merchants. Thank you for the offer though."

The two met again sometime after the church bell rang for None. Henry brought wine, which the creature had found he could drink without ill effect. Not for him was the escape of grape or grain when he was troubled. When they each had a glass in their hand, the creature said, "Tell me of my father's life, who is he and why did he make me?"

"When young, Victor suffered the loss of loved ones and so became obsessed with overcoming death. When Augustus Darvell was murdered, Victor sought to bring him back. Darvell's body was too damaged, so he put his brain into the body you now wear."

Henry went on, telling the creatures of Victor's experiments and of the elixir and the spark of life.

"So I am, in a fashion, immortal, even if I die. I need only someone to ignite the spark of life within me."

"Possibly," Henry said in a manner that caused the creature to remark,

"You are a clever man, M. Clerval. And I suspect you are thinking of how you would kill me should I threaten my creator or his family." Without waiting for a denial, the creature smiled and asked, "Tell me, what method would you try."

Returning the smile, Henry said, "I do not know if I should tell you, but you have had ample opportunities to do the Frankensteins harm and have not availed yourself of them, or so you say." He paused, then, "I would behead you, remove part of your skull, and destroy your brain. Or I would just burn your body. I do not think you could recover from either."

The creature considered this then laughed. "I do not think so either but take care that you do not wind up with a mindless body or a pile of intelligent ash and bone."

Henry joined in the laughter and refilled their cups. "Tell me about your life so far."

The creature told him of his become aware, his life in the woods, his meeting of the De Lacey family, their tragic fate, and his terrible vengeance.

"I had heard of the death of Étienne Defreyne. So it was you who killed him?"

"I was happy. I had the family my creator had denied me. The soldiers and this Defreyne took them from me."

The two had talked so long that the bell for Vespers began to ring.

"I must go," Henry said. "Same time in two days?" When the creature hesitated he added, "Fear not. I can keep a confidence and I care nothing for men who would slaughter a family. Nor do I care much for the law. The laws of Geneva and of the Church would condemn a man like me faster than a murderer. Murder they understand, my kind they do not."

"For what do you care, M. Clerval?"

"I care for justice and those I love."

Two days later, again after None, the two met in the ruins. The creature came last, after making sure that Henry had come alone.

"Tell me of this girl you and my father resurrected." After Henry told him the sad tale of Justine Moritz, the creature said, "The confession bothers me, that is, her denial of it. Why would this girl, knowing she was likely to go to her god, risk her immortal soul by recanting?"

"It could be that the Calvinist priest lied to curry favor with the magistrate."

The creature shook his head. "By confirming what was already believed. And although I do not understand this division in your faiths, why would this Calvinist care for the soul of a Catholic, who by his beliefs is already damned because of hers. I can think of only one reason."

Henry considered the creature's words for a time, then,

"My God! You do not mean. But that is monstrous!"

"My father may have been right. A monster did kill his brother, but not one of his making."

"But how can we be sure?"

The creature stood. "I have some ideas on that matter. But do not worry. I will not act unless I'm certain."

"And when you are?" The look on the creature's face was all the answer Henry needed. "It is a sin to kill a man of God, whatever the offense."

"Sins are for those who have a soul, and I am not sure that I have one. You will hear from me, Henry Clerval."

43

Seeking work, the creature presented himself at the residence of Reverend Gerber. He was met by the priest's serving-man. "I do most of what is needed and hire for the rest. You look strong enough. Where can you be found?"

"Alas, I have nowhere to rest my head. I often sleep rough unless payment for the work I find includes a roof over my head while I do it. What tavern do you frequent? I could stop in from time to time. I would be grateful for any jobs you could give me."

"How grateful?"

The creature paused as if in consideration. "A tenth of what I am paid."

The manservant shook his head. "A fifth, and for another fifth, I will include bread and wine."

"Given for whom you work I would think that bread and wine would be free. But I accept."

The manservant named a tavern. "Come tomorrow night. I may have something. I may have work for you, but it may not be for the priest."

"And for whom do I ask?"

"I am called Igor but use that name quietly and do not shout it."

"Until tomorrow night, Igor."

The next night, the creature stopped at the ruins then found the tavern which Igor had named, but he did not enter. Instead, he stood in the shadows, the hood of his cloak over his head, and watched and waited. He watched Igor enter, waited for him to leave, the followed him.

The streets in that part of Geneva were dark. There were no lamps to guide people to their homes. Whatever light there was, was provided by the moon and stars and the torches sold on the corners by children who had no home or family. Many of those who walked the street had no money for torches, especially after visiting a tavern, and so risked the darkness knowing that anyone who wished them harm would be suffering under the same handicap as they.

But for one. The creature's vision was far better than most and even in near-total darkness he saw as if it were twilight. He followed Igor long to make sure that he himself was not followed, then accosted the man and dragged him into an alley that smelled of garbage and human waste.

As he felt himself lifted into the air, Igor tried to scream but a strong hand around his neck stopped his voice. It relaxed enough for the manservant to ask, "Wh …what do you want. I have no money on me, nothing for you to take."

"You have your life," came a harsh whisper. "Which I would willingly take. I have questions for you."

Along with his eyesight, the creature's hearing was better than the average human. He could plainly hear Igor's heart thumping in his chest. "I am going to put you down. If you try to flee, I will snap something so that you cannot. Do you understand?"

A croaked "Yes," and Igor was placed on his feet.

"What do you want to know?"

"Wait, calm down a bit. You will not suffer unless you lie. And I will know if you do."

The creature waited until he heard Igor's hear slow its beats. "Tell me of the Reverend Gerber and what he does to children."

Igor was surprised by the question. His heart sped up a little, then he again calmed. "I do not know what you are talking about."

As the lie started, his heart racing again, he felt the creature's large hand on his shoulder near his throat. "Are Gerber's sins worth dying for, Igor?"

Igor apparently decided that they were not for he said, "He uses them for his pleasure. Mostly I get them for him, either off the streets or from parents who have too many to feed. He uses them. When he's finished, I … dispose of them. This is an old country, there are many dry wells."

"And young Frankenstein, what of him?" Another squeeze of encouragement, this time at the base of the throat.

"My master is … the Frankensteins are Catholic, he had little contact with them. He did not recognize the boy. He tried to entice him, the boy struggled. His death was an accident, or so he said."

"William Frankenstein died so that he could not denounce the priest. Why take the portrait?"

"So that he could place the blame on another. He gave me this task to me. I saw a girl sleeping in a barn. I placed it in her pocket. "

"Very well. I thank you for your honesty."

"So I may go?"

The creature's "No," sounded out in the alley like a death knell, which in a way it was.

"But you said you would spare me, show me mercy if I spoke the truth."

"I said you would not suffer. I made no promise about your life. As to mercy …"

The creature's hand moved quickly to snap the neck of the manservant. "Compare to your master's fate, this is mercy."

Leaving Igor's body amidst the trash and waste, the creature made his way to the residence of Reverend Gerber. Moving quietly in the darkness, he entered the home then soon left it carrying the gagged, chained, and unconscious body of the priest. He then made his way to the tomb of the family Frankenstein. The church bells were ringing out Matins as he finished digging out the unused grave of Justine Moritz.

When the priest awakened the creature told him, "I know about the children. I know of your murder of William Frankenstein. I know of your lies that killed Justine Moritz." He took off the gag. "Is there anything to say before you die condemned for your sins?"

Chained as he was, Gerber still managed a shrug. "My sins do not matter. No man's do. One is either of the elect or not. As a minister of the Lord I hope to be among the former. So kill me and send me to the salvation of God."

Again the creature gagged him. "I have studied your belief and while I do not believe as you do, I cannot be certain that you are not correct." Taking out a syringe, the creature injected the priest with the elixir. "This will keep you alive as you lie in the grave meant for your last victim. As I shovel the dirt on top of you, you will struggle to break free, but the chains are strong enough to hold me, so you will not break them. You will lie awake buried in the earth and suffer the pains of hunger and thirst. You will lie there as the worms and insects begin to feast on you. What they do not devour your own body will in its effort to maintain itself. Eventually, maybe months or years from now, the elixir may fail and only then will your face your god. Pray that your belief is real, for if it is not, then your suffering will have only begun."

The creature then pushed Gerber into the open grave and began shoveling the dirt on top of him. When he was done, he made sure that it showed no signs of having been disturbed.

His task complete, the creature stood for a moment, listening. He had dug the grave deep, three or four feet deeper than most graves. So deep that not even his hearing could detect the sound of a chained man screaming into his gag.

44

The following day, Henry Clerval again met with the creature. "Reverend Gerber's manservant body was found in an alley outside a pub. He was dead."

The creature nodded. "I know. I killed him."

Henry said nothing. He had suspected as much. And with the creature's admission, he was afraid that Victor had been correct as to his nature.

"William Frankenstein was not the first of Gerber's victims. He used children, M. Clerval, used them to satisfy his lust. The manservant procured the children and disposed of their bodies once Gerber was done with them. Igor's death was too swift, too merciful, He should have taken longer to die."

There was an unsettling look on the creature's features as he spoke of the manservant's death. "And what of Reverend Gerber? Is he also dead?"

"Do not call him 'Reverend.' A man such as he is a worse monster than I. Yes, M. Clerval, I believe that I may be a monster. At the least, there is one inside me. I did not enjoy killing the soldiers who slaughtered my family. But I must confess to a certain thrill as I crept into the home of Étienne Defreyne, as I held him down and slowly squeezed the life from him, as I wished him to Hell as he died. I enjoyed that very much. As I enjoyed snapping the neck of Igor. And when I think of Gerber's fate I smile, knowing that it will be a long time before he meets his god, if he ever does."

"My God, man, what did you do to him?"

"Do not call me 'man', for I have to accept that I am not one, nor can I ever be. Thanks to my father, I am something new. As to Gerber's fate, that is for me to know. Were I to tell you, you may seek to free him and so you would, like my father, release a monster into this world. All I will tell you is that he is in a much deserved living hell."

Henry looked at the creature and did not see a monster. Rather, he saw a man in pain and sought to console him.

"I believe that there is a monster inside us all," he said. "Those men who killed Fritz and Augustus Darvell, they gave way to their monsters. Many men do, and for poorer reasons than you had. We must try to keep the monsters inside us."

"And what if I cannot?"

"I believe you can. Consider this, I know of your existence and I know how to destroy you. I could rally enough men to hunt you down and put an end to you. Yet, knowing this, you have not attacked me. It may be that you are not the monster you think you are."

"I would pray that you are right, M. Clerval, if I had a god to whom I could pray. But I must be off."

"Where are you going?"

"I think you know. I go to Mont Blanc to find my father. I want to know why he abandoned me and ask him for the answers a son is due from his father."

45

Victor Frankenstein had a lead of several days on his creation. Yet Victor did not have the creature's stamina. His ascent of Mount Blanc was more difficult than he had expected and each day the creature came a little closer to him.

Just as the elixir in his body had reacted to that in Justine's, so did that which ran through the creature's veins lead him to his father. With each step along the correct path, he felt his bond with his creator grow stronger, and it lessened should he make a misstep. It was only a matter of days, days without food and nights without sleep, that the creature caught sight of the man he sought and followed him to the summit of Mont Blanc.

As the creature reached the top his creator turned and recognized him.

"I know you, foul creature. I know you for the devil you are, an evil spirit who possessed the soul of the good man I was trying to restore to life. I know you for the killer of my brother and for causing the death of Justine Moritz. Begone, lest I destroy you."

"You could try, Father," the creature said calmly. "But I doubt you would succeed. I tell you that I did not kill young William. His death was at the hands of others who even now are in the cold ground, for I have avenged his death."

"You lie, you monster. I saw you in Geneva. What business would you have there but to take vengeance on me through my family?"

The creature sighed and sat on a rock. *I should have expected this,* he thought. *For if he sees me as a monster then he is absolved of the guilt of abandoning me. But I must try.*

"Before you judge me, Father, let me tell you of the life I have led."

"I do not care to hear it."

"Yet you must. For if you try to leave, I will prevent you. So listen, then judge me."

Again the creature told the story from his awakening to the deaths of the De Laceys, the soldiers, and Étienne Defreyne.

"So you confess to being a murderer. How do I know that you did not kill that man and his family, then murder the soldiers when they discovered your foul deeds?"

"The deaths of the soldiers and Defreyne were just punishment for their having killed the only family I have ever had."

"You are not a man and so have not right to judge men. I may have created you but your real father is Satan."

"And is Justine a child of the devil as well? Yes, I know of her resurrection. I watched you and M. Clerval restore her to life. Is she fated to also become a monster?"

"No, she was but a child and by not having the courage to denounce you I was partly responsible for her death."

"Yet she was convicted of your brother's death. A holy man even exposed her confession. Why believe in her innocence but not mine? Is it because she is beautiful and I am hideous?"

To this Victor had no reply. It was not something he had contemplated. He was not sure he would like the answer. Instead, he stood facing his creation for a time, as if debating whether he should attack him or flee from him. Finally, he said,

"What do you want from me?"

"Just what any son is due from his father. I wish a name and a future."

"You are not a man and so deserve no name. As for your future, I care not."

There is no reasoning with him. So if it as a monster he sees me, then I monster I will be.

"Have you considered, Father, that if what you say is so, that if I did kill William and the rest, then their deaths rest with you. You fled from me and when I mindlessly escaped, you did not seek me out. You left me without the guidance a father should give his son. Any crimes I may have committed are the result of your neglect."

Victor began to shake his head in denial but before he could deny the charges the creature continued.

"Consider this, Father. You believed that I killed William out of hatred for what you did to me. If this is so, then why do you assume that the rest of your family is safe. I could return to Geneva this very day and slay your father Alphonse, your brother Ernest, your friend Clerval, and even your cousin Elizabeth. They will be dead and beyond resurrection by the time you arrive. You will be forever left alone for I will destroy anyone you love or who dares to love you."

Victor rushed at him. His hands raised to strike. The creature grabbed his wrists and easily held him. "I could do this, but I will not, for I am not the monster you deem me to be. I want only one thing from you."

"And what is that," Victor asked.

"If, as you say, I am not a man then make for me a mate, one with whom I can spend my life. Do this and we will go far away, to the Indies or to America. We will live alone on what nature provides and you need never worry about us again."

"And why should I?"

"Do this and your family is safe." *They will be safe either way, but he does not know this. If he refuses, he will forever worry that one day or night I will strike, and that would be enough for me.*

When the creature released him, Victor moved several steps away from him. For a moment, the creature thought that he might throw himself from the summit as if his death would prevent those of the ones he loved.

"Very well," Victor finally said. "But not here, not in or near Geneva. I need a quiet place to make you a bride. My family has a villa at Lake Como. I will go there. Give me a few months then seek me out. You found me here, you can find me there, for now I know what the strange feeling that came over me as you approached was. The same elixir that is in you is in me."

The creature smiled. "We are bound then, like father and son."

"If so, then I renounce you. I will do what you ask and afterward want nothing more to do with you."

"I give you six months, Father. After that, well, when you leave your family, be sure to bid farewell to them, for you may never again see them alive."

With this the creature began his descent, leaving his creator alone and afraid.

46

Fr-rom the diary of Elizabeth Lavenza
On Victor's return from Mont Blanc, he kept his promise and we began to plan our wedding. He told me several times that he could not wait until we were united in marriage and physically as well. There were times when we embraced that I felt his passion for me and I hinted as much as was proper that we did not have to wait to please one another and that there were ways by which any unwanted consequences could be avoided. He confessed that while he yearned for me, he wanted our union to be a pure one, us joining together in our marriage bed in love rather than pre-martial lust.

I do not understand that. Love is love even if it is not blessed by a man in black who supposedly has never known a woman. Why did God give us the ability to please one another if we have to wait to do so? I, for one, do not wish to wait and if it were not for the possibility of the scandal that caused my mother to be cast out of House Frankenstein, indeed, to lose the name of Frankenstein, I would not wait but go impure to my nuptial bed. If Victor is as pure as he claims he would not know of a ghost on our wedding night.

Instead, I content myself by my own hand but it does nothing to still my yearning for the intimate touch of a man.

Victor seems worried. When we are out walking, he is constantly looking around, as if watching for someone or waiting for something to happen. At home, he frequently looks out on the grounds. Sometimes I look out with him but see no one. One evening I heard him discussing with Uncle Alphonse the disappearance of Reverend Gerber and the murder of his man Igor.

"There is a monster out there, Father," he said, "One that preys on men. We best take care."

"That was over a month ago, Victor. Given where Igor was found it's likely that he was killed in a drunken brawl. As for Gerber, the fewer of Calvin's followers in Geneva the better."

"Still, Father, I think we should hire more men, to better guard the house. And arm them and the ones we already have."

"To have them shoot at shadows in the night and maybe wound an innocent? No, I do not think so, Son."

"As you wish, Father." But after Uncle Alphonse left the room, I saw Victor go to the window and clearly heard him say, "I know you are out there, watching me. I will go when I'm ready and not before."

Go where, I wondered, and to whom was he speaking?

I think that Victor's concerns are rubbing off on me for I have several times now seen a stranger crossing our lands. He does not approach the house but instead pauses and looks up at it as if he is imagining what it would be like to be inside. Many people do I am sure, the envy of the lower classes for their betters, but this one seems different.

I saw him closely one day. I was returning from town when my carriage passed by him. Of course, he stepped off the road to let me pass. As I did, he bowed then smiled as if he had a secret to share. There is something about him, something primitive. He is tall, very tall with long, dark hair. His face is scarred to the point of ugliness but rather than repulse me it intrigued me in some way. I have perhaps, been reading too many of those romances of which Uncle Alphonse disapproves. I thought to mention him to Victor but was afraid that it would only fuel my fiancé's worry about intruders. Instead, I kept my sighting of this man to myself.

I have seen him again, the brute of a man who bowed to my carriage. Once in town, I saw him from across the street. Again he smiled and bowed, as if he knew me and I should have known him. The second time was when a friend with whom I was having lunch mentioned that someone was staying in Reverend's Gerber's now abandoned home.

Against all reason, I knew this to be the large, dark-haired man. As Victor was away with Uncle Alphonse on family business, I asked Ernest to take a walk with me. We passed the cemetery where I paid my respects to poor Justine, then I steered us toward the Gerber house, There I saw him, chopping wood against the coming Fall. Despite a slight chill in the air, he was bare-chested and I could see that his chest, like his face, was also scarred. On seeing us he covered up, much to my disappointment.

At my urging, Ernest approached him. They spoke for a time and when my cousin returned to me he said that the man, whose name he did not get, had been hired to prepare the house for the arrival of Reverend Gerber's appointed successor. "He said that Henry Clerval got him the position."

I resolved then to ask Henry about him. It may be that he was one of Henry's "special friends" but there was something in the way that the man looked at me that made me doubt this.

My closeness to this man, my near obsession with him, caused a certain tension within me. That night, as I sought to relieve it, the image of the large, dark-haired, man, with his scarred body stripped to the waist, came unbidden to my mind as I achieved satisfaction.

Victor is leaving me again. He told me last night that he and Henry will be traveling to the English Isles to consult with scholars in his field. He could not or would tell me the purpose of this consultation, informing me that I would not understand.

I fear I understand all too well. He does not love me and his talk of desired intimacy is simply that, talk. I even suggested that on the night before his departure we give each other a farewell gift and made it clear that this gift would be the sharing of our bodies. As usual, he demurred and I begin to suspect that his desires are more akin to Henry's than they are to those of most men.

Victor will be gone for several months he tells me, and Henry along with him. I will be alone in this house with only my uncle, my cousin, and the servants for company. There are my friends, of course, to occupy my time. And there is also the large dark-haired stranger who is increasingly in my thoughts and dreams.

47

Frm the journal of Victor Frankenstein
The monster of my creation has become my nightmare. What had been a quest to free mankind from the embrace of death has brought the threat of that death to my family. The foul beast demands that I make another like him, a mate to satisfy his passion. Unless I yield to his will, he will murder those I love. He killed my brother and caused the death of dear Justine. He will do the same to my father, my brother Ernest, my friend Henry, my fiancé Elizabeth. And only the Devil knows what perversions he will inflict on her before he grants her the release of death.

He forces me to choose. To save them, must I condemn the world to another like him? And if I do, what then? Will they procreate and thus begin a race of beings that could supplant humanity? They may, for the elixir running through their veins makes them stronger, faster, and less prone to injury. I see them among the savages in North America, learning their ways, their knowledge and superiority making them like gods to those primitives. And like all gods, they will demand obedience of their followers and form them into a crusading army to drive the Europeans back into the seas from whence they came.

Or would they hide themselves in the jungles of South America, breeding there in secret for generations, breeding and not dying until an entire race of homo monstrums emerge to sweep mankind away in a flood of murder. I cannot do this, yet how can I not, knowing that my family is at risk.

He watches me, the beast of my creation. I see him walking the grounds, staring up at the house. I feel him as well. When he gets close the elixir that runs through his veins calls out to that within me. At night I stand on my balcony, the same one from which I watched the storm, the damned storm that inspired me when I sought dominion over death, and I know that he is out there. He haunts me, yet he is a ghost I cannot put to rest. I am in agony, yet to the others I must pretend to be happy and gay. The only time that is true is when I talk of love and marriage to Elizabeth. My body yearns for her love in all its aspects. Sometimes at night I burn with need and consider her offer of surrender. But no, I dare not touch her until all is over, not until the monster has departed and my family is safe. For should she get with child it will only be another hostage to the beast, another victim of his lust for death.

I slept well last night, the first good night's sleep since my return from the mountain. I have solved the problem. I will make for the creature a bride but use the knowledge taught to me by Augustus Darvell to fully remove her internal organs of regeneration. It must be a full removal so that the elixir cannot repair the damage I will do. There will be scars, but as I intend to make his bride as ugly as he is, he will not notice a few more. It is justice in its way, using the knowledge of Darvell to thwart the designs of the one that has his brain. It is the only way to save my family and the world itself.

I see him on a daily basis now. I believe that he has a lair someplace close from which he watches me.

It is time to leave. Last night when I went to my room, I found the balcony doors ajar and a note affixed to my pillow by the knife I use to open letters. The one word written on it, "When?" spoke volumes. It told me that he could enter the house when he chose, and if he could enter my room he could enter any of them. I panicked, thinking that maybe he left another message somewhere else, one written in blood. Running from my room I woke the house, making sure to account for everyone.
Of course, they looked at me as if I were mad, and it is likely that at that moment I was. On my father's inquiry of "Victor, what is the meaning of this?" I answered,
"Forgive me, Father, but I was standing on my balcony enjoying the night air when I thought I saw someone enter the house. I roused the household lest we be robbed and assaulted in our sleep." Of course, I did not tell him of the note.
Father ordered a search but nothing was found disturbed.
"Did you see this intruder, Victor," Ernest asked. He was a man of action and had answered my call armed with his grandfather's sword.
"He seemed a tall man. In the moonlight I could see that he had black hair and may have been scarred."
"Really, how interesting?" my cousin said, then she smiled in a way that seemed to be incongruous with the situation. She left us and repaired to her own bedroom. Father then directed a search of the grounds that turned up nothing.
Just a note this time, and while there was an implied threat to my

family none were harmed.

The bells were chiming Matins before the household was settled. As I lay down to sleep, I heard my balcony door creak open. I looked up to see a large moonlit shadow outside it. A whispered voice said,

"If I can get to you, Father, I can get to her. Your choice, my bride or yours." He then asked, "When?" and was gone.

I ran to the balcony but could not see his monstrous form. Certain he could hear me I said, "Within the week." Then I closed the door and blocked it with a table.

When morning came, I was still awake. The next evening the nightmare returned, nightmares of him and Elizabeth. And damn me but there were times when I woke from them aroused.

He shall have his bride.

48

"I thought we were going to Lake Como?" Henry asked Victor as they prepared for their journey.

"That is what I told the creature, Henry. I needed to get out from under his stalking eyes. He watches all the time now. At night I lie awake expecting to hear the cries of my family. When I do sleep it is with the knowledge that he is outside my window. When I awake, I expect him to be standing over my bed."

"I thought the elixir bound you, that you could sense one another."

"He is clever, as clever as the Devil who is his true father. He has found a way to mask it. But I have fooled him. We shall depart for Lake Como as I told him but instead we will continue to Genoa and from there take ship for the British Isles. There are some scholars I wish to consult in England. From there to Scotland, where I will find a quiet place to do the devil's work so I can be rid of him."

"And how is he to know where to find his bride?"

"When I revive her, she will be as a child. I will bring her to him."

Henry could see several paths by which Victor's plan could go astray, but he did not want to challenge his dearest friend. Victor's mind seemed to be in a fragile state and the wrong word could cause a breakdown. Perhaps it was fortunate that he was leaving the country.

"You need not accompany me."

Henry shook his head. "You may need my help. Lake Como sounded like a restful getaway. But your plans are now more of an adventure, perhaps our last one. When we return you shall marry Elizabeth and have no time for your unmarried friends. And soon I will be taking on more and more responsibility for my father's business. So one last trip together, my friend, and may it be successful."

"I pray that is so. I pray that next year this time the long nightmare that began in Ingolstadt will be over. Once the creature has his bride, I will rid myself of what elixir I have remaining, destroy the metal netting, burn my journals, and repent my sin of Pride that caused me to dare defy the sanctity of death."

They boarded the *Star Tender* in Genoa. It was a Greek ship that was to take them to Britain though the Strait of Gibraltar. Its master was Captain Galen Manikas who, despite his naming, was as wide as he was large. He was a good-natured man, although hard on his crew when they failed to live up to his expectations. Which was often.

"You are descended from heroes. If you had been aboard the *Argos* the Golden Fleece would never have been found. Had you sailed with Odysseus he would have given himself over to the sirens rather than sail with you. Now show our landlocked passengers how a proper ship is handled or I swear by Poseidon himself that I will make port in Marseille and replace you with French pornés. They won't be much use sailing but by Zeus, we'll at least enjoy ourselves before we all go down."

"They'll go down before the ship does, Captain," countered the first mate.

"Only if you pay them well, Nikos," replied Captain Manikas, "and on what I pay you, all you'll get to do is watch."

The captain was glad to have passengers on his ship. It meant that there were those on board who had not heard his stories. It was a way for him and Victor to occupy their time.

Henry, who had been on ships since he was old enough to accompany his merchant father on business, occupied himself by working with the crew. And there were a few sailors who were interested in occupying themselves with Henry.

"You know, of course?" Captain Manikas asked Victor over a bottle of *tsipouro* which the captain laced with anise. The captain liked drinking with Victor, amazed at the younger man's tolerance for strong drink, little knowing that it was the Elixir of Life flowing through Victor's veins that kept him from getting drunk.

The *Star Tender* had just passed through the Strait of Gibraltar, which Captain Manikas insisted on calling the Pillars of Heracles. He had just finished telling his passenger of how the Greek hero Heracles, not to be confused with the Roman imposter Hercules, smashed through the mountain of Atlas and so joined the sea with the ocean.

Victor took another sip of *tsipouro* and nodded his head. "We have been friends since boyhood. We have no secrets from each other and we have secrets that no one else knows."

"And are you ..." He nodded meaningfully toward Henry.

"We have shared many things but not that. Is ..." it was Victor's turn to nod meaningfully, "... this a problem?"

Manikas shrugged. "Some men are, some are not. Some are but only on board ship. It matters as not as long as the ship sails smoothly. If it does not ..." Again the captain shrugged. "But a word of warning, my friend. The isles to which we sail, they are not so tolerant. They are ruled by the church more so than other countries. Tell him, no, warn him to be careful, for his sake as well as yours. For if you two are traveling together, what befalls one will befall the other."

The *Star Tender* arrived in Liverpool on schedule and with no problems – no storms, no pirates, no sickness.

"For the luck you brought us, you may sail with us anytime," Captain Manikas said as Henry and Victor disembarked. "And remember my warning."

The belongings and equipment unloaded, Victor and Henry went to an inn where they stayed a few days exploring the borough.

"The sea voyage seems to have done you good, Victor."

"I am calm away from Geneva and … him yet I dread traveling north to do his bidding. But for now, I'm off to Cambridge where I hope to review papers left them by Newton. And you, I know that you did well on our voyage." At Henry's smile, Victor added, "Just remember the captain's words and be discrete, or be chaste."

"I'd rather be chased than chaste, Victor, but I will be careful. But mostly I'll be about my father's business, first here, then in Ireland. He wants me to explore new markets."

"Then we must soon part, my friend. My 'business' should take but a few months. When complete, where shall we meet you?"

"The town of Belfast, I think. Let us meet there in three months. I plan on taking rooms at the Giant's Ring."

"Until then, my friend and be careful."

"Until then. And I will."

49

When the Reverend Casper Reinsfelder arrived in Geneva to assume the responsibilities of the still missing Reverend Gerber, he was surprised to find that his house was not attached to his church but lay just outside the city. It was modest abode in comparison to the other houses around it, but it was near the woods and private enough that there would be few parishioners bothering him at all hours.

Even better was his discovery that the house and grounds were well kept. *I was told someone was to look after the place*, the reverend thought just as that someone came from behind the house.

On seeing the man and taking in his height and the scars on his face and torso Reinsfelder's first impulse to flee at the monstrous apparition. But as if knowing what the priest was thinking and feeling, the man smiled and approached, holding his hand out in greeting.

"Greetings, Reverend. I wasn't expecting you until next week."

As the man's huge hand enveloped his, Reinsfelder replied, "My work at my old post was done, so I decided to come early." *Not a monster*, the reverend decided, *just a large man whose ugliness is not his fault, though there are some ministers of the Lord who would think otherwise.* "You were Father Gerber's man?"

The man shook his head. "I did not have that honor. His manservant was murdered shortly before your predecessor's departure. To be honest, there are some who think the latter was due to the former but who can say? No, it fell to me to maintain the house and grounds until a successor was appointed."

"Will you be staying on … Forgive my manners, I am Casper Reinsfelder, and you are?"

That is a good question, the man thought. *One for which I do not have an answer. What if I told him the truth, that I am the created son of Victor Frankenstein, a creature possibly not known to God. Shall I tell him of my birth and abandonment? And would he bless me or curse if I did? But he needs a name from me. Well, this body once had one.*

"Call me Fritz, Reverend. And if you do not have a man of your own, I will glad to stay on for a few months. Then I think I will be moving on."

"A wandering sort, are you Fritz?"

The creature shrugged. "My life often forces me to be so. At times is it as Luke says, 'Foxes have dens and birds of the sky have shelters, but this son of man does not have a place to lay his head.'"

"You know your Bible then?" asked the reverend, apparently surprised that a member of the working class could quote scripture.

"I have read it. Can anyone say that he truly knows it? But come inside, Reverend, I believe there is enough food for a decent meal. Tomorrow I shall go into town and see you properly provisioned."

"Thank you, Fritz. Will you join me?"

The creature would, beginning to like this man who seemed different from the one who was no doubt still screaming beneath the earth. *Or maybe not*, he thought. *It must be difficult to scream through a gag.*

The creature prepared and served the meal. Grace was said and the two men ate.

"Are you of the Faith, Fritz?"

The creature shook his head. "No, I am not. Nor do I follow Rome. But from what I know of your faith that should not matter. One is either saved or not."

"In a way, Fritz. I believe that the Creator sees the past, present, and future all at once, and so knows what choices men will make to save or damn themselves."

"If he knows this, why does he not prevent our sinning and so save us?"

Reinsfelder paused to look at this strange man, a man with the face of a monster, the body of a worker, and seemingly the mind of a scholar. He began to wonder to what purpose he had been sent to Geneva and why this man had been put into his path.

"Without free will, we are little more than animals. With it, we are free to choose our own. That the Lord has already seen what paths we have chosen does not lessen the fact that we have chosen them."

When dinner was done, the creature showed the reverend the bedroom.

"And where do you sleep?"

"Not here, Reverend. For now, this son of man has a place in the wood where he lays his head. With your leave, I will go there. Tomorrow I will go into town to set up your accounts and order whatever you might need."

"Thank you, Fritz, but I will do that. I have to visit the church, my church now, and this will give me a chance to meet the townspeople."

"As you wish, Reverend."

Taking his leave, the creature went to the ruins where Justine had been revived and where he had met Henry Clerval. There was something about it that reminded him of his cave in the woods and so he had made it his home. And so had the cat that had once rubbed against his legs, its scars long since covered by fur. Occasionally, the feline would even deem the creature worthy to be allowed to pet it.

As he lay on a bed of blankets that he had taken from Gerber's home and which he was sure that Reinsfelder would not miss, he thought about what had been said over dinner.

So if I am a monster it is by my choice and no one else's, not even my father's. If I thought that God would listen to one such as me, I would pray that I will never again have to face that choice.

He was, however, certain that if God heard his prayers, His only answer would be that that was a choice he would have to make again and again for as long as he lived, which might be a very long time indeed.

50

With Victor gone, Ernest training with the guard, and her uncle spending more and more time with the Genevan Council, the management of House Frankenstein fell more and more to Elizabeth. After the death of her aunt, Elizabeth had become accustomed to overseeing the household, but now the grounds became her responsibly as well. Her friends having moved on, either to school or into marriage, she welcomed the work. It lessened the time she was lonely. However, there were still many hours in the long day when all there was to do was read, play music, or simply stare at the window and wonder. She'd wonder what Victor was doing, and with whom. She wondered if he was being as faithful to her as he said. She began to resent him for these imaginary offenses that may or may not have been. When would Victor return? Would they be married when he did? Or would he find another excuse, another journey he had to make. Another excuse to avoid her, to avoid their future together. Did Victor even love her, she wondered. Not that his love truly mattered. After all, she did not love him. She'd do her duty by him and hoped he'd do his duty toward her. They'd produce and raise heirs so that the Frankenstein name could continue. And yet, there were times she wondered why it should. Would the world be better or worse if Victor never returned and Ernest was killed fighting, and she never married but became a childless spinster? Would the world mourn? Or would it even notice?

But there were times she did not think of marriage, children, or of House Frankenstein. No, she thought of her life as it was and of her dreams and desires and how neither were fulfilled. And in thinking of these things her thoughts strayed to the pleasures denied her in her current state. Yearnings unfilled, yearnings sometimes hinted at and sometimes explicitly described in some of the novels by anonymous authors she'd taken from her uncle's study without his knowledge.

Elizabeth would read these works in bed by candlelight, pleasing herself afterward, even knowing that such pleasure was but a pale imitation of true passion, a poor substitute for the arms and loins of a lover who truly desired her.

Afterward, she would sometimes dream. Sometimes of Victor, sometimes of Henry, but mostly of the dark-haired man.

Since seeing him working at Reverend Gerber's home, Elizabeth made it a point to pass by there frequently on her trips to town or her inspections of the estate. Sometimes she would see him, other times not. When she did, and he saw her, he would bow and smile. When she did not see him she'd wonder where he was – in the city getting supplies, in the house preparing a meal, or in the woods hunting for dinner. And she'd wonder if there was a woman with whom he spent time, spent it with her the way she dreamed he would with her.

She would tell herself that he was ugly, that his scarred face and chest (and who knew what else) made him ugly, and that she had no wish to be with such imperfection. But it was his ugliness that drew her to him, that made him different from the perfumed dandies who fluttered around her at the balls and galas. There was more attention in his bow and smile than an hour of tepid chatting and dancing. Or so it felt to her.

She reminded herself that he was a common worker and probably uneducated. Such a man was not worthy of a lady, much less a Frankenstein. But she did not desire him as a husband and the reason for which she did desire him had nothing to do with where and how or on what side of the blanket he was born. For was she not born on the wrong side of that same blanket?

She did not want to make her mother's mistake. Her mother was careless and was caught out. For that reason, she told herself, she should entertain the dark-haired man only in her thoughts and dreams. But there are ways, her baser needs told her, ways described in her uncle's books, ways spoken of among her friends, times safer than others. And there was Onan, who sinned against God and his sister-in-law by spilling on the ground. *A small sin to have so enraged the Lord*, she thought, and one she would willingly commit with a partner who was not her husband.

Elizabeth began to think of the dark-haired man in her every waking hour when she was not otherwise occupied. Desire became obsession and she knew she wanted him closer to her. Even without excuses, she would ride by the new reverend's home in hopes of catching a glimpse of him. If she saw him on the streets of Geneva she would dismiss her servant and follow him. She had to have him closer, and she imagined that he felt the same about her. And if not, she knew she could make him feel that way. Her books had shown her how that could be done.

51

He noticed her of course. Noticed her increasingly riding by Reinsfelder's home, noticed her watching him when she did so. The creature had seen her in town and was sure she had followed him, and while he forbore to turn around to make certain, he did amuse himself by taking circuitous routes to extend her chase.

Why? he asked himself. Why him when there were so many who were more pleasant to look upon. This question sometimes led him to think back to his time in the woods outside Ingolstadt. He'd think of the De Laceys, especially Agatha and how he felt toward her. She had not shied away from him and it may be that she would not have rejected his advances if he but had the courage to make them.

Elizabeth Lavenza – he had learned her name from Henry Clerval before the man had gone off with Victor Frankenstein. And at times he would think of her as she thought of him. She was a beautiful woman, as beautiful in every way that he was not. And while he wondered what might happen if he dared approach her, would she scream and flee or would she remain and smile, she was not his. She was his father's, the bride-to-be of Victor Frankenstein. In addition, he would soon have his own bride, if his father were true to his word.

And if he is not, he sometimes asked himself, *what then? Will you honor your promise to him and slay his family one by one, leaving him as alone as you?* It was then he thought of Elizabeth and knew whatever else he might do, he could never destroy such beauty.

52

"Fritz, a word please."

"Yes, Reverend?"

"Are your duties here such that you can spare time from them?"

"For what purpose, Sir?"

"For a request from the lady of House Frankenstein."

On hearing this the creature felt as if his heart had skipped a beat and he unconsciously held his breath for a second. Reverend Reinsfelder noticed this and suspected the cause – he was not unobservant – but chose to say nothing.

"A request for what?"

"She sent a servant with a letter asking if you may be spared from your duties for a day or two. There's some land she needs cleared. Her regular servants are all engaged in other work and in her letter she asks if I might lend you to her. Not that you are mine to lend. Unlike what is happening in the Americas. A terrible sin it is, for one man to think he can own another. There will be an equally terrible punishment for such a sin, which I doubt will completely wash the stain away. And so the choice is yours. If your work here can spare you and you wish to work for Elizabeth Frankenstein …"

"Her last name is Lavenza. She is a cousin of the Frankenstein and engaged to the son Victor."

"And you know this how?" Reinsfelder asked.

"From Henry Clerval. I was doing work for him," the creature explained, silently adding, *punishing your predecessor*, "during which he told me of the Frankensteins."

"A lovely lady," remarked Reinsfelder.

"Yes, she is," agreed the creature in a somewhat thoughtful voice, as if picturing Elizabeth's loveliness, "but not for such as I."

"I have learned many things in my three decades of service to the Lord, Fritz. One of them is not to judge from outward appearances. I sense a nobility of spirit about you that even you deny."

The creature gave a harsh laugh. "I may be other than I appear, Reverend, but noble I am not. But tell me, what else have you learned?"

"That it is the woman who decides who is worthy and once she has decided, will not be gainsaid. Which may present a problem if the woman is of one class and the man of another."

"Such as the lady of an estate and a common laborer?"

"Exactly such. Society frowns on such liaisons. While there may be passion and pleasure there may be no future. However, since the Lord God lives all times at once, he knows your fate and so your destiny is set. So I suggest you accept your fate, however unpleasant or pleasant it might be."

I have known happiness, but never the passion or pleasure of which he speaks. As for my future, I doubt if I have one. And so,

"You may be right, Reverend. So if you would, please send a reply to the Lady Lavenza that I will be at her service the day after tomorrow and for the next few days after that."

He reported to the Frankenstein estate and was put to work clearing land that did not appear to need clearing. When that was done, he helped the other workers as best he could. He was large and strong and he could lift heavy things and so his help was welcomed. No one questioned his presence. No one suggested that it was for any reason but to help around the grounds. At night he stayed with the workers of the estate rather than return to the ruins which were his home.

She watched him. Watched him clear the fields, watched him work with the animals in the barn and stables. He was good with them, she noticed. His strong hands treating them gently but firmly. She imagined him treating her in a like manner.

He knew she watched. He felt her eyes on him. At times he would look toward the house and see her in the window. At times he thought to wave and might have if there had been no one else present.

At the end of four days, she sent for him, meeting him in the rear of the house outside the servants' entrance.

She was, to him, more beautiful than she had appeared from far away. Her hair beyond that of gold, her eyes bluer than the sky. Her face was as perfect as his was not. His senses aroused, he heard the rapid beating of her heart. He inhaled her scents, the perfume she wore not masking the natural aroma of her body and beneath them both a musky smell that called to him as a man and caused his body to respond.

Not since Agatha, he thought.

He was larger than she had supposed, his body towering over her. His face was scarred as if someone had long ago taken a blade to him. She wanted to touch his scars, to trace them with her fingers and then continue with those on his body.

How many does he have, and where else might they be on his body.
She wondered about his body and if all of him was as large.

His eyes were clear, sometimes green and sometimes grey, and they looked at her in a way that suggested she had no secrets from this man.

When she greeted him, he did not bow as did her servants but instead smiled and his teeth shone white in his mouth.

"Thank you for your help," she said. She handed him some coins and in doing so, touched him, her hand lingering on his longer than would be considered proper. It was he who, reluctantly, pulled away.

"It was my pleasure, my lady. If you … have need of me again, leave word with Reverend Reinsfelder and I will come … attend to you."

"And if I do not wish to leave word with the priest?"

He sensed her heart beat faster, her aroma grow stronger. He himself began to ache. *So this is passion,* he thought, and smiled again at its painful pleasure.

"Then you will just have to find me, my lady."

A challenge, a dare, and both knew it.

"I just might, Fritz. Will you be returning to the priest now?"

"No, I live … elsewhere." But he did not tell her where. Instead, he stepped away and this time did bow. "My lady," he said and was gone.

53

Elizabeth watched and waited. She waited at a distance from Reverend Reinsfelder's home and watched until she saw him leave. She followed him as he went into the woods. In time, she knew where he was going and did not follow him any longer.

He knew she was there. He caught her scents on the air, the smells of her perfume and of her body. He did not detect her secret aroma, the one that had in its way spoken to him on the day they parted. Knowing she was following, he did not confront her. Nor did he attempt to elude her. He had hunted before, for the De Laceys. He knew that sometimes you must let your quarry come to you.

Days past. He concentrated on his work even as he watched for her. He did not see or sense her. *She's lost interest. She's found someone else. She's come to her senses and has decided that her beauty is such that she could not bear to be with his ugliness. It's for the best for both her and me.*

He told himself other things as well and sometimes believed them all and sometimes none of them.

Each night he would return to the ruins. He'd wash in a nearby stream, eat what he foraged from the forest, and read until his candle was almost gone. Then he'd sleep and hope not to dream of her. For however sweet the dream, when he awoke he was always alone.

Six days after their parting, after their bodies spoke what they could not and would not admit, he returned from the stream. As he dressed, he thought he heard a noise outside the ruins. An animal perhaps crunching leaf, snapping dry twig. When the wind shifted his way, then he knew it was no common beast.

He whispered into the darkness. "Lady Lavenza, should you be out so late? It is not safe to be about in the dark."

She stepped into the candlelight as if she were ethereal, too exquisite to be real. For a moment he reasoned he must be dreaming, but even in his wildest fantasies he could not have imaged a vision of such bewitching beauty. The illusion of her being otherworldly was broken when she opened the bullseye lantern which had guided her way. The brighter light made it clear that she was real, yet in no way diminished her alure. "I played here as a girl, with Victor and Henry. These woods hold no danger to me. I trust that is still so."

"It is, my lady. I see you found me. Have you… need of me?"

She did not answer his question. Not with her words at least. That she needed him, wanted him, was clear to both of them, even if neither yet had the courage to acknowledge that need that held them both in its tender and teasing grasp. Instead she shown her light around his living quarters. Gasping in surprise, she said, "Books! I see you read."

"Yes, I have most of my life. I am no ignorant brute as some may think, good for nothing for clearing, lifting, and hauling." The creature did not hide the gentle curl of his lips into a sly grin.

"I never thought … no, that is not true, Fritz. I did think that of you and did not care, wanting only one part of you." There was no need to speak of which part. Even unspoken, it dominated the shadows and everything else between them. "Forgive me." Bringing her light closer, she looked over his books. Some she recognized from her uncle's library, some of which she had read. Others she had heard about but had never seen. And some …

"Who is this Perrault?"

"A teller of tales, my lady, imagined stories for children with lessons for both them and their parents."

"We have such books at home, some of which were read to us as children and others, others that are more suited for adults. There is one that tells that of a young girl who, in order to save her father, agreed to become the companion, the intimate companion to a horrible beast. She was afraid but agreed to surrender her virtue to him anyway."

"And what happened?" the creature asked.

"The beast was taken by her grace and beauty and fell so in love with her that he did not force himself on her. Rather he waited until the night she came willingly to his bed. The next morning when she awoke, she marveled at the handsome man beside her."

"I see." The creature could not hide the disappointment that colored his words. No mere act of love or passion would ever turn him into ordinary looking, let alone handsome. If that was what she was expecting, Elizabeth would be sorely disappointed.

"No, Fritz, you do not. The beast's appearance did not change. Instead, she saw his inner beauty."

Whatever else may have happened that night was interrupted by the church bells tolling compline.

"It is late," he said.

"Not too late," she protested. "There is time."

He knew what she was suggesting, what she was offering. It

meant everything. Still, he said,

"Not enough. There are times for haste but this is not one of them. Go home for now." Elizabeth did not move, did not budge. She could not, would not. Her every night's desire was before her, close enough to make real with the gentlest of touches. She would not deny herself that which she had waiting for so very long. She looked at the giant before her and was ready to convince him to do that which she knew they both desired. That was her plan, at least until he said, "I think I would like to read that story. Perhaps you could bring it the next time you visit, say tomorrow at the tenth hour?"

She caught her breath, only realizing then that she was panting, the filling and emptying of her lungs keeping pace with her racing heart. Her voice came out deep and soft, unable to hide her desire. "You will be here?"

"Waiting for you to come to me," then dared to add, "my beauty."

"I will," she replied, "my beast."

Elizabeth left, having no need of the lantern to find her way. The creature, as happy as he had ever felt, followed unseen and saw her safely home.

The following night Elizabeth came willingly to him. He had wine, though they did not drink it. She brought the books of tales she had mentioned. They did not read any.

There were far more important matters to attend to.

Slowly, she undressed for him, revealing herself with each piece of clothing she removed. She reveled in the expression of awe and reverence on his scarred face. He felt adrift in her beauty. Finished and as unencumbered by clothing as the day she was born, she simply stood and watched him look at her as though she was the most precious person in the entire world, which had somehow shrunk to encompass only the two of them.

Transfixed, he stood unable to look away from the splendor laid bare before him. She lay down upon his bed of leaves that had only a blanket to cover it. To her it felt finer than the finest mattress. To his senses, her want and desire were undeniable.

It was now his turn. He undressed for her, revealing himself more with each piece of clothing he shed. Normally, he would be self-conscious at his scars and coarse appearance, but beneath her hungry gaze, he felt the acceptance his father and the rest of the world had eternally denied him. When he was finished, he simply stood there, his want and desire now obvious, Elizabeth looked at his scarred body and found him beautiful. Then he lay down next to her.

In whispers, they told each other what they liked, how they pleased themselves so that they could please each other. Soon he heard her sigh in passion and she felt the urgency of his body. "Now," she whispered and they joined together.

There was pain and pleasure and soon she cried out in delight. His moment quickly followed hers and so together they became lost in the sweet mystery of physical love.

Afterward, their desires sated, they held each other. They drank the wine and read the book. "Tell me of yourself, Beast."

He longed to tell the truth but knew he could not. Instead, he told of being abandoned by his father and later being adopted by a family, a family that was now dead.

"Since then I have been alone."

"Until now. Whatever comes, you will never again be alone. I will always be with you."

"And I you. And what of you, Beauty?"

Being the bastard child of a Frankenstein was not something she wanted to share with him. Instead, she spoke of how her noble mother was cast out and why, and how she was also adopted only to lose her beloved aunt and her cherished mother.

On hearing of her mother's plight, he said, "We must be careful."

"Yes, we must." In her uncle's books she had read how and so told him.

Two nights later they met again. After their fiery passions were spent, she showed him the book she had brought. In it was a work called "The Wife" by the poet Thomas Overbury. When she read the verses:

> *So God in Eve did perfect man, begun;*
> *Till then, in vain much of himself he had:*
> *In Adam, God created only one,*
> *Eve, and the world to come, in Eve he made.*
> *We are two halves: whiles each from other strays*
> *Both barren are; joined, both their like can raise.*

He stopped her.

"I have been called by many names, none of them mine for my father never named me but to call me monster and creature. I use what name is convenient. Until now I have called myself Fritz after a man I once knew. But after tonight, and our previous night together I will be called Adam, for you are the Eve who has completed me."

"Then, my dear Adam, while the rest of the world calls me Elizabeth, to you and you alone will I be Eve, although while together like this you will still be beast to my beauty."

And seeing that his desire has returned, she put her book aside saying, "And now I shall ride my beast."

And so she did and when her passion crested she called out "Adam" and when she granted him release he whispered out "Eve."

54

A week went by and then another. They were not together every night but they met every night they could. They read, drank wine, and made love. But there finally appeared the shadow of a serpent in their paradise, one that grew more and more solid until thoughts of it could no longer be ignored.

"What of Victor?" Adam finally asked.

Her face in the candlelight answered him before her words could. "I love you, Adam, but I am destined to be Lady Frankenstein. When Victor returns from Britain, we will be wed. I am sorry." As she said this, there was hurt and pain in her voice which was mirrored in his reply.

"I have always known this. I too have a destiny which I must follow and perhaps sooner than we both would like. But let us enjoy what little time we have left, my Beauty."

"Yes, let's, and speaking of enjoyment, let us finish this night as we started, my Beast."

55

From the journal of Adam Frankenstein

My father lied to me as to his destination. Had it not been for Eve's words I would have thought him in Italy. Instead, he has fled to the British Isles.

"Come find me," my father said the one and only time we spoke. Very well, in this, I will be a dutiful son and obey him. I will leave my love, my Beauty, my Eve, and travel to north to find him, trusting the elixir's bond to track him down. By then he should have made for me my own bride and if I feel for her a mere tenth of how I feel for Eve, I shall be a happy man.

56

From the diary of Elizabeth Lavenza

My love has left me, as he said he must. Yesterday I went to our ruins only to find them abandoned but for a note.

"Eve," it read,

"As I told you last night, my destiny calls. As much as my heart will miss you, it is time that I answer it. It will give you time to prepare for Victor's return. The pain I will feel knowing that you will be with him will be lessened by my memories of you, and each time anyone calls me 'Adam' it will bring to mind how your love baptized me.

"Farewell, my Beauty. If it is as Reverend Reinsfelder says and that we cannot escape our Fate, if we are meant to be together again, we shall be.

"Your loving Beast, your Adam."

Last night I cried for Adam. Today I begin to again to live without him. I have neglected my duties to the house and grounds and though I think some of the servants may suspect why, none would dare speak, not if they do not wish to suffer the fates of the two who informed on poor Justine. I also have a wedding to plan, and a wedding night. I cannot give Victor the gift which a bride should give her husband, but he does not need to know this. If his words to me are true, then he will come as an innocent to our bed and so should be easily fooled. As I had to surrender the man I loved in sacrifice to our marriage, I will have no regret in taking Victor's innocence, should he have any. If he does not, then his sin shall cancel mine. Until then, I will think only of the future and try to forget the past. However, should Fate again bring Adam and me together, I pray that Victor again will be easily fooled. Or suitably distracted.

57

From the diary of Henry Clerval

I worry about Victor. Except when he was with Captain Manikas, he was sullen throughout our entire voyage. When we did speak, all he spoke of was his monster. No, having known him I cannot call him that. Rather I'll write "creature" but I feel even that does him an injustice. He seemed as much a man as anyone, with faults and virtues. I confess that his punishment of Igor and Gerber caused me a few sleepless nights, but if any men deserved punishment they did.

I do not know if the threats from this son of Victor Frankenstein were made by him or if they are the product of my friend's fevered imagination. Or if they were made to prompt Victor to create a mate. We all yearn for one, a companion with whom we can spend our days. My parents had each other, Alphonse Frankenstein had Caroline, Victor will have Elizabeth. I hope Victor can create someone for the creature. If so, maybe I can have him make one for me. I jest, but it is the bitter truth that such relationships are not for those such as I. One of us might be tolerated as long as we remain single, but two, no. Then would the churchmen and the magistrates lead the angry townsfolk to our door to drive us out or worse, treating us as bigger monsters than Victor thinks his creation to be. I do believe that given the choice between a resurrected man and two men in love, they would welcome the creature and drive the lovers out, possibly into separate unmarked and unhallowed graves. Perhaps if I ever find someone dear to me, we could move to where no one knows us, one to play the master and the other the servant. Until then, it is quiet assignations in dark, forgotten places.

I take ship for Belfast in the morning. I look forward to being at sea again, although I do not expect it to be as enjoyable as my journey on the Star Tender. Men of my own kind, never have I been happier. Perhaps when this journey is finished, I will go to sea again, tending my father's business. But for now, I prepare for Ireland.

I've been at the Giant's Ring for two weeks now and have never been busier. There is much to do in this port, discovering which men want to buy things from Africa, India, and the Ottomans and which men have wares to offer. I will write my father and obtain his permission to use the letters of credit to which he entrusted to me to purchase goods, hire a ship and crew, and begin a new life as a seagoing merchant. I hope Victor, when he comes, does not mind returning home alone.

There is trouble and I may be in the middle of it. England may rule the country of Ireland but it does not rule her people. 600 years of English rule has led to many uprisings and with the memory of the Great Frost and the resultant famine there looks to be another. There is talk of an Act of Union that will merge the two countries into one, effectively ending even the pretense of Irish independence. I had heard rumors of a growing United Irishmen movement that strives to prevent this from happening, rumors that became fact for me when I was approached in the tavern the other night.

I was approached by two men, neither of whom gave me their names but I had heard some whisper "Liam MacTire" when the larger of the pair walked in, although the epitaph of the Wolf of Belfast was a bit troubling.

"We hear that you are looking to establish trade in and out of Eire," one said.

When I allowed that was true the other, MacTire, asked, "Would you be opposed to some quick trips to France to bring us needed … tools? These trips would put the ready into your pocket and finance your further trips."

It is not good to get involved in politics and rebellion, and I had no doubts that what I would be bringing in would be tools of war. Putting the rumors together with the fact that France is the traditional enemy of England I declined the offer.

MacTire smiled, revealing incisors reminiscent of a wolf's. Perhaps that was the source of what the other patrons called him in their whispers, but I suspected not. "You don't understand, Henry, our asking was only us being polite. You will do the job, or we'll find someone else, and one day someone may eventually find you, or what's left of you."

"But I don't even have a ship."

"You will, a good one if a bit on the small side. And you'll have a crew, all good men above suspicion, at least for the next year or so."

"If you have a ship and crew, why do you need me?"

"For your good looks, of course. And the fact that you're foreign and more above suspicion than the crew. You'll get a share a when it's all over plus the ship to sail where you please."

I considered agreeing then leaving Belfast quietly, but I had no way of contacting Victor, who in a month or two would come to the Giant's Ring asking after me. And then these same men would take out my betrayal on him. And so, God help me, I agreed and so became a part of what some have since called the "Patriot Game."

And little did I imagine how very descriptive the name Wolf truly was.

58

Despite the fact that his thesis received only lukewarm praise from his professors in Ingolstadt, Victor Frankenstein was well received in Cambridge by Edward Waring, who, like Isaac Newton, was a Lucasian professor of mathematics.

"I must confess surprise that you've even heard of it, Professor, much less read it," Victor said when Waring welcomed him to Magdalene College.

"Oh, we get them all, Frankenstein. Cambridge employs scores of young men whose only task is to obtain copies of papers written by scholars of lesser universities. Oh, forgive me, I do not mean that as a slight upon Ingolstadt. It is a very ... fine place. I meant lesser to Cambridge, of course. Come to think of it, I would suppose that all are lesser to Cambridge, although Oxford does come close, as perhaps one day that colonial school Harvard may. Your paper managed to cause a minor stir, what with the general thought of the new chemistries replacing the old. Your studies showed how the new sciences could not have succeeded without the philosophers and alchemists who came before."

"What was it that Sir Isaac said, Professor, that he only succeeded by standing on the shoulders of giants. I think now many are standing on his shoulders and seeing even further."

"An excellent point, Frankenstein, one, with your permission, or even without it, to be honest, I will make myself at some later date. Now then, let us have dinner and you can tell me how we may be of service."

It was over drinks following an excellent repast that Victor requested access to Newton's private papers and research.

"What is it you seek?" Waring asked.

"Why, the Elixir of Life and the Philosopher's Stone, of course. I wish to become rich and immortal."

The was general laughter at what the company thought was a joke on Victor's part. When it died down, Waring said, "I find wealth to be overrated, young man, and from what I can see, most men spend far too long upon this earth."

"I agree, Professor. In truth, having read his public writings I wish to know Sir Isaac better, to study what private journals and notes are available so as to further guide my future endeavors."

Waring looked around the room, seeking a consensus. He was many nods and no shakes of the head. "Very well, Frankenstein, you may begin in the morning. The usual rules, of course, notes only. Nothing is to be removed. And you are to send us a copy of whatever you may publish. Agreed?"

Victor agreed and began work the next day.

It took him a month to find what he sought, Newton's original notes on his *Calculus of Creation*. On reading them, Victor was surprised by how close Sir Isaac had come to finding the elixir, much closer than his public work had indicated. There was mention of the use of something Newton called "Royal Jelly" as an activation agent and outlines for experiments similar to those Victor had conducted but after these plans there was nothing, as if Newton had simply abandoned his research.

Why, Victor asked himself, *when he was so close*? He had to have known.

The notes were dated and so Victor sought out Newton's diaries and journals for that time. He found no answer. Nor did he expect to. All of Newton's works had no doubt been examined by the best minds of Cambridge and elsewhere and while none were his equal, they would not have missed Newton's declaration of success or failure on the preservation or restoration of life.

But there had to be an answer somewhere. If not in his papers, then maybe his books. Comments and notes in their margins, perhaps. But which book? His time was running short. He had a monster's bride to create if he was to save his own. Then Victor asked himself, *What is Royal Jelly*?

He soon found that Royal Jelly was created when a certain bee species ate the pollen from certain rare species of plants. Victor looked over the books left by Newton to Cambridge. There were several on Botany and just one on Apiology. He looked through the latter first and found what he had been looking for.

There was a paper in Newton's hand.

If you have found this, it read, *it may be that you are very interested in bees. If so, read on and forget this note. If, however, you have sought this volume for another reason, then heed my warning. Abandon your efforts now, before you commit my sin. I once thought to challenge the Almighty in His creation. Using the essence of a man I made a homunculus, one no larger than the elves of Ireland are said to be. I learned too late that what I had made was an evil, soulless thing. There were deaths in Cambridge that could only have been caused by the thing I made. It was only through God's Grace that I captured and destroyed it. I also destroyed my notes which is why the ones you found seem incomplete.*

There is Good and Evil in this world. And the latter is not a person, or a demon, or an Angel fallen from Paradise. No, it is a great Void. Pride and hubris lead us to its edge and if we do not turn back we are certain to fall.

I urge you, you who are reading this, to turn away from this Abyss lest the gravity of Evil pull you into its darkness. And if you do not, may the Divine forgive both of us.

For a time, Victor sat and looked at the letter, the warning from one of the greatest minds the world had ever known. *Would that I had read this earlier,* he finally thought. *No,* he then realized, *I would have dismissed the warning, certain that I knew better, that I would succeed where Newton could not, that my view from his shoulder would show me a better way.*

But now, instead of standing on Newton's shoulder, I stand on the precipice of the Abyss, where the voices of those who have fallen into it call out to me to join them. Little do they know that I already have, and, despite Sir Isaac's prayer, there may be no forgiveness for me. For I have made one monster and now to save those I love, I must create another.

The next day, after thanking Professor Waring for his hospitality, Victor Frankenstein left for Scotland and the city of Perth to begin his work on a bride for the creature. In his pocket were pages he had cut from one of Newton's notebooks and a letter he had found in a book on bees.

59

"But why Perth?" Henry had asked Victor before they had left the *Star Tender*. "There's nothing there, nothing that's not in abundance here in Geneva."

"Trust me, Henry. There is something in Perth that I need. And do not forget, *he* is here. He stalks me. He haunts my dreams. To do his bidding, I need time away from him. Besides, Geneva is too close. People know me here. The things I must do for *him* are best done where I am a stranger to men and they to me."

"Strangers are suspect, Victor."

"Do not worry, my friend. All will be well."

The "something" to which Victor had referred was in actuality a "someone," Albert Gaffner, also late of Ingolstadt, one who had attended M. Darvell's anatomy lessons. Gaffner was Scottish on his mother's side and had finished his studies in Edinburgh. He now taught the natural sciences at Perth Academy where he also continued his anatomical research.

Victor and Gaffner had continued their friendship by post after Gaffner was asked to withdrawal from Ingolstadt. (There was a scandal involving him, a barmaid, and the daughter of one of the history professors.)

As you know, my friend, Gaffner had written in a letter that Victor received just after his return from Mont Blanc, *the difficulty in studying the human form is the obtaining of subjects to examine. There are women who, for a price, will allow "in-depth" external examinations along with other more personal services but I am but a poor teacher – no, make that an underpaid teacher for I feel that my teaching skills are better than most – and cannot afford such research more than once every few weeks. And the people here are very respectful of the dead, there is nothing like the charnel house in Ingolstadt where one could obtain the odd specimen for an internal examination.*

But as we were taught, there is a solution to every problem, even if that solution is water and fortified wine. Not long after my arrival at the academy, I was approached by a man who asked if I was in need of "biological specimens." When I inquired as to the nature of the specimens he could provide he became evasive, hinting that they were such that were not readily available. When he mentioned that his cousin was an undertaker, I came to understand his meaning. Since then he has supplied me with several "specimens" at a reasonable price. Fortunately, in addition to my paltry salary, I am allowed a certain amount with which to purchase educational supplies. I do not question how he obtains these specimens but I suspect that at times some families buried rocks and sacks of flour rather than their loved ones and that other times the deceased are "resurrected" in much the same manner as the poor girl that was the cause of Darvell's death.

I hope your own researches are going well. If fate ever brings you to these northern isles please come for a visit. It will be good to see you once again and perhaps we can again work together.

On receiving this letter, Victor immediately replied to make arrangements for a visit. He had been concerned about the obtaining of a suitable subject for the monster's bride and this appeared to be an answer to the dark prayers that he had been ashamed to utter even to himself. While at Cambridge he received confirmation of the planned visit and so left for Perth with only the problem of how to revive the body without his friend becoming aware of what he was doing.

He considered this on the long coach ride to Perth. He had the needed supplies with him – the thin, metal netting, a collapsible Franklin rod of his own design, and a fresh supply of the elixir. The chemists at Cambridge were more than happy to provide Professor Waring's special guest with whatever he needed and it had given Victor special satisfaction to mix the life-giving potion where Newton and taught and studied.

With supplies at the ready, Victor only needed someplace to perform his dark deed. He would decline Gaffner's offer of hospitality and seek quarters somewhat outside of Perth in order to perform some "special" research. This would no doubt lead his friend to suspect that he was the kind of man who enjoyed making free with the bodies of dead girls. But to Victor, it mattered not what his friend thought. He'd not see the man again and would thereafter refuse to engage in further correspondence.

These thoughts, these plans to sacrifice a part of his reputation to do what was needed caused Victor to think back to when he, M. Darvell, and Fritz were standing over the dead body of Anna Felder just before cutting into her. Despite the fact she was dead, he had been aroused by her nudity. And then there was Justine. Again, he had felt himself harden when he and Henry removed her covering and exposed her naked body, warm and breathing thanks to the elixir.

That night, as Victor lay in a not very comfortable bed in a roadside inn, he dreamed the dreams of a lonely man. He did not, as he sometimes did, dream of Elizabeth but rather of Anna and Justine, and when he woke in the morning he found that his body had responded messily to the things he did to them in his dreams.

60

Victor was greeted by Albert Gaffner who took him to his academy quarters. "Only one bed, I'm afraid, and not a very large one. I don't suppose …"

Victor shook his head. "No, is there someplace just outside of town. I like quiet nights."

There was, and Victor soon moved into an old farmhouse. The owner had failed as a farmer and now rented out rooms by the month, the week, or the day.

"Or the hour," Gaffner informed his friend on their way there. "It's one of those discrete places that everyone knows about but no one mentions. Mostly they pretend it doesn't exist, which seems like a perfect place for your … experiments, if you're still interested."

"I am. Do you … experiment there?'

Gaffner shook his head. "There are more or less forgotten rooms in the lower levels of the academy. There are rumors that either arcane rituals were performed there or that they were the lair of a *nosferatu*. The kind we once believed the poor, unfortunate Darvell to be. Better for him if he had been. No one goes there and so it's perfect for my work. And before you ask, Victor, I don't dare share the space with you. The presence of a stranger at night might lead to discovery."

"I understand. Let us keep our secrets to ourselves, Albert. What we don't know we cannot reveal."

The rooms allotted to Victor were perfect for what he intended. Like his apartment in Ingolstadt, there was a bedroom, a living space that would serve as a study, and a spare room where he could work. Best of all, it was on the ground floor and had its own entrance.

They're fine," he told the farmer as he paid for a month's lodging. "I trust that I won't be disturbed," he said, dropping a few more coins into the man's hand.

"No one will know you're here, sir, unless you tell them."

"Fine, and one more thing. Do you get many storms this time of year?"

The one-time farmer nodded. "We do. It's the season. Why, are you bothered by them?'

"On the contrary. I welcome them. They are exciting to watch."

Victor declined Gaffner's invitation to return to town using his long journey as an excuse. Before they left, he asked him,

"Have you heard from our mutual friend?"

"I will see him tonight. For what are you looking?"

"A woman of marriable age. Not more than four or five days gone."

"I'll see what he can do. Tomorrow then. I'll give you the tour of the town and academy. Then we can drink, toast each other, and tell lies about our time in Ingolstadt."

That night in a pub not far from the Perth Academy, a man came in and without ceremony sat at Victor's and Gaffner's table.

"Two days from now," the man whispered. Then to Gaffner, he said, "You know the place." Then to Victor, "Hope you don't mind fresh."

Victor shook his head. The man made him uncomfortable. He seemed the sort to be featured in the broadsides sold at hangings. And how did he know that something "fresh" would be available in two days? Maybe there was to be a hanging or two. They did that a lot on this isle, he had heard.

The thought of a hanging brought to mind Justine's death, and that caused Victor to again remember her warm, naked body. He would have another rough night if he did not take care of himself before going to bed.

The man's "Half now," took Victor out of reverie. Victor handed him a coin-filled pouch. "Allow me," he said to Gaffner.

His friend nodded his thanks, smiled, and said, "Then I shall get the next round and the one after that. And you, Lee?"

Gaffner turned to where the man he had called "Lee" had been sitting but like a devil who had just dealt for a soul, he was gone.

The meeting place was a clearing not far from the farmhouse where Victor was lodged. As arranged, he and Gaffner arrived just after sunset.

"Can we trust this man?" Victor asked.

"He's not played me false yet."

Gaffner's "yet" did not reassure Victor. What did was the charged pistol he had in his pocket and the long knife he wore at his side. As a scion of House Frankenstein, he knew how to use both. A pity he did not take them to school with him. Perhaps he would have had the wisdom to have ended his creation before its escape.

"Was there a hanging today?" he asked his friend.

Gaffner shook his head. "No, why do you ask?"

Victor's "Never mind" was drowned out by the noisy approach of a horse-drawn cart. Lee was driving, In the back were three others, two of whom were hooded and bound. When the cart had stopped, the man riding in the back threw the prisoners to the ground.

"What is this?" Gaffner demanded.

Lee replied, "Don't worry. These two won't be missed. You said you didn't mind fresh. They don't get fresher than alive. Conrad, if you will?"

Conrad pulled off the hoods. The smaller of the two was a boy of maybe twelve or thirteen. The other was a young woman of maybe eighteen.

"Nice, aren't they? And I think the girl is very fresh, if you get my meaning. You can have a bit of fun before you do, well, whatever your kind do. You just have to decide which of you goes first."

"But they were supposed to be dead." Even as Victor spoke he knew his protest would be useless. But he did not expect Lee's reply.

"Have it your own way. Conrad."

The other man drew a knife, ran it across the boys' throat, causing a large gout of blood to come gushing out. At the same time, Lee put his knife to the woman's throat.

On seeing what was happening, Victor reacted instinctively. He drew his pistol and fired at the closest target – Conrad. As the man fell backward, Lee let the woman fall and attacked Gaffner, ramming his blade into the teacher's abdomen. Dropping his pistol, Victor attacked Lee. His assault was quick, a knife in the back followed by a slash to the carotid artery. Lee fell, bleeding out on the ground.

What has just happened? Victor asked himself. *Three dead and,* he checked the woman, *one much of the way there. Save who you can.*

Victor dropped his knife. If stopped, he did not want to have a weapon on him.

I had taken a walk, heard a noise, investigated, and found them. Concerned for the woman, I put her in the cart and was seeking help.

That was the story he would tell if stopped. He put the woman in the cart and led the horse from the clearing. But then,

She may not survive the journey back to town. I could save her. I have the elixir, I could inject her, revive her, and make her like me.

And so he returned to the farmhouse. Hiding the cart in the barn, he made sure there were no watchers, then carried the woman into his apartment and laid her on the table of the workroom.

Her breathing was ragged. By lamplight he saw that her skin was very pale and that with every heartbeat, more of her lifeblood pumped from the gash on her neck. The elixir was at hand. With one injection, he could save her as Henry had saved him. He reached for it, but his thoughts forced his hand to pause.

True, he could save her. But alive she would be a person with no future. ("Don't worry," Lee had said. "These two won't be missed.") Dead, she would be the bride he needed, the salvation of his loved ones. One life, an insignificant one at that, in exchange for several, more important ones.

He stared at the dying woman. To his surprise, she was still conscious. Unable to speak, her eyes implored him to help her. Maybe she saw Victor's answer in his eyes. Maybe she did not. Perhaps she heard his whispered, "I'm sorry" and perhaps she did not. It was not long until her eyes glazed over, and she saw nothing more.

Looking down at the newly dead body of the woman he had chosen not to save, a great weariness overcame Victor. But he had no time to rest. Tomorrow, or perhaps the next day, the bodies would be found. Maybe the authorities would believe they had killed each other and take no further action. Maybe they would find marks from the cart which would lead them to the barn, the farmhouse, and him. He had to leave. He gathered his clothes and equipment and carefully wrapped the woman's body. Placing all in the cart, he headed north, away from Perth and the hue and cry that would seek a killer.

Away from Perth, a voice in Victor's head, perhaps his conscience, reminded him that there was still time to save the dead woman. That he could bring her back the way he had Justine. He ignored this voice, as he ignored the other one that called him beast and monster.

She would not really be dead. Or that's at least what he told himself and the voices should they stop speaking long enough to listen. Instead, her body would reborn into a new life. But he knew this to be a lie and knew himself to be as much a monster as his creation. The voices in his mind did not disagree.

No, he thought, *not as much as he. For he is the one who has driven me to this. The creature is the monster, not I, and it is on his head as well as mine that the guilt for this woman's death lies. But no matter, if to save my family I must be a monster then very well. I will be a monster. And woe be to any who get in my way.*

61

From the diary of Henry Clerval
I was contemplating a way to sneak away and then find a way to get a message to Victor, but it was not to be.

As the best way to disappear from Belfast was by sea, went to the docks in hopes of securing passage on a ship leaving in the morning. I did it at night figuring that members of the United Irish would be less likely to spot me than in the light of day than by the light of the moon.

I figured wrong.

As I got to the docks, a voice from the shadows spoke to me.

"Not planning on leaving yet, Henry me lad?"

I instantly recognized the voice as MacTire's but the shape in the shadows looked nothing like the man. Or a man at all. Well, it was upright, with two arms and legs, but it appeared to have pointed ears, an elongated jaw that was filled with sharp teeth, and was covered in thick brown fur. MacTire looked like a wolf who had learned to imitate a man.

I tried telling myself that it was a trick of the shadows, that such things couldn't be. But then I thought of Justine and Victor's creature. If the dead could be revived, then anything was possible.

"Of course not. Just out for a late night stroll." The thing that was MacTire was polite enough to do no more than glare at the bag I carried over my shoulder, but it was too big to hide either it or my real reason for being there. Still, I did not wish to end up as MacTire's snack so I tried anyway. "Perhaps see if I can find that ship you had told me about."

"I will take you to see it on the morrow."

"Not tonight?" I am not sure why I said that. This beast of a man had instilled terror in me, far more than Victor's creature ever had. I wanted nothing more than to be away from here.

"Tonight I am on the lookout for a spy of the British. 'Twas only luck that I spotted you. The docks are a dangerous place at night. It is not uncommon for a man walking alone, especially one treading where he should not, to disappear into the ocean forever."

His threat was unspoken but abundantly clear. "How terrible. I suppose I should hurry back to my room then."

"Yes, that would be best. It would be a shame if something should happen to our new partner."

I don't remember how I got to my room as my next memory is of locking the door. And the thought that I best purchase some silver.

I saw the ship the next day.

The Rover, *for that is the name of the ship I was given, has made three trips so far. Each one has followed the same course. First to The Netherlands, where we unload our cargo and pick up brandy, tobacco, and the arms needed by MacTire and the United Irish for their rebellion. Then to the southeast coast of England. We unload the brandy and tobacco at a place called Romney Marsh in exchange for gold which will be used to support the rebellion when it comes. If it ever does. I have my doubts about some of the so-called rebels. They seem no more trustworthy than the "Night Riders" who receive the smuggled goods under the watchful eye of their strangely clad leader whom even MacTire defers to. Some of the men with whom I sail and nominally command seem more interested in the gold than the freedom of Ireland. Still, the trips have been profitable. And MacTire has assured me that that the next trip will be the last, that next time we make part in Belfast the* Rover *will be mine. It will be nice to surprise Victor with my very own ship in which to return home.*

The surprise, at it turns out, was mine, and it was not a pleasant one. It began one night last week. I was alone in my room in the Giant's Ring where there came a knock on my door. I opened to find a beautiful, redhaired young lady. I had seen her before in the tavern and had noticed that she usually left with one or the other of the men there. Whether she left for pleasure or profit I could not say and did not care. Standing at my door, she asked to enter and made a suggestion that if I were not otherwise inclined I might have accepted, regardless of the price. As it was, I thanked her for the offer then, citing religious reasons and a fiancé waiting back in Geneva, declined the lass's offer with seeming regret, stating that the best I could do was dream of her that night. She said that I was sweet, then leaned over and kissed my cheek. As she did so she pressed something into my hand. As soon as she left, I barred the door and looked at the paper. It was a note, which bore an address, a time, and a warning. "Come alone. Make certain that you are not followed."

It was not from the rebels. They had other ways to contact me – a word in the tavern, a whisper from the shadows, a nod and a wink at just the right moment. Anyway, the Rover *would not need to sail for a few weeks.*

I examined the note. Written on quality paper in a fine, educated hand. As I thought, not the rebels. It was likely that someone was on to us. At first, I thought to tell one of the mates onboard the Rover then thought better of it. They had made sure I had heard about what befell those who betrayed the cause. Then I thought to keep the arranged appointment but again, decided not to. If it was from whom I thought it was, like the rebels, there would be no turning them down.

I burnt the note.

Not deciding is in itself a decision and in what is now the light of the morning I know that I should leave Belfast as soon as I can by coach. I could stand losing the Rover and my profits but Victor will be looking for me at the Giant's Ring. If I had a way of posting him a message I would, but as it is I can only pray that he arrives before the Rover is again set to sail. Then we can jump ship in Holland and make our way back home by land. I know I stay at risk to my life but I cannot abandon Victor and, should he succeed, the Bride.

I wonder about the girl, the redhaired one that handed me the note. What part does she play? Was she hired to the errand or is she in league with the sender? Maybe her carnal activities are for more than, as I write above, pleasure or profit. Maybe in the aftermath of passion spent she asks questions and received answers from those who unwittingly betray their comrades. In truth, it does not matter. Each night before I fall asleep I pray that Victor will arrive the next day only to be disappointed and then pray the prayer again.

A knife held to one's throat is a wonderful attention getter. This night I was walking to the tavern when I was grabbed and rushed into an alley. One man held me while the other placed a sharp blade against my neck.

"You missed the meeting," the man said, pushing the blade against my skin.

There was no point in denying it. The woman would have told of its delivery. "I did not wish to be robbed. I have heard of such things happening."

His answer was to first remove the knife. Then he punched me hard in the stomach. Had the other man not been supporting me I would have collapsed.

"Listen carefully. We know about the United Irishmen. There are as many spies among them as there are thieves and patriots, though there are precious few of the latter. My name is Captain Collyer and *what I want are the smugglers of Romney Marsh, especially that damned Scarecrow who leads them. Tell me the where and when and I'll let you and your 'rebels' leave before my men move in. Or they can find your body in this alley tomorrow morning, or in a few weeks should you lie to me."*

I learned that night that I am not a brave man. I thought I was, but after another punch followed by the return of the knife to my throat, I told all I knew.

The time for sailing is getting close. Please come soon, Victor.

62

From the journal of Adam Frankenstein

When I left Geneva, I walked until I came to the waters that separated the continent from the British Isles. It was a long trip, traveling during the day, sleeping at night. I've found that I don't really need much sleep but I enjoy the quiet and restfulness of the night. Not that the night is noiseless. There are creatures about that know better than to trust to man's kindness for their survival. Maybe like them, I should sleep away the day and travel by night. But men, or even such as I, cannot do that without being suspected of ill-intentions. So as I traveled, when the sun went down I foraged for my food, found a secluded spot to enjoy it, and slept.

And dreamed.

Sometimes I would dream of the De Lacey's only to awaken and remember their fate. Sometimes I think I dreamed the dreams of the man I used to be. Maybe nothing is lost and somewhere in my mind this Darvell cries out to be freed, or at least heard. These dreams inevitably lead me to consider a false priest buried deep in a young girl's grave. Is he still gagged or has that long since rotted away? If so, did he try to cry out for help only to have his pleas muffled by a mouthful of dirt? I am not man enough to forgive him and pray for his salvation. But I am monster enough to hope that his suffering endures for decades if not centuries.

Most often, I would dream of Elizabeth, my Beauty whom I now call Eve, and our time together. I dreamed that that time is not over but will come again. Sometimes when I awoke, further sleep eluded me and I could not help but wonder why I was making this journey when what I wanted and needed was behind me.

I know the answer, but there is in me enough of a man to look for ways to change it, to change her so that, if the bride of Frankenstein she would be, it would be as my bride, and not his.

But whether asleep or awake, these dreams are just that, dreams. I may have delighted in her body first, but she has chosen to give it to another. She has made a choice I must accept.

As I write this I am waiting for the ship that will take me to England first, then to Scotland and so to my father, and my bride.

My bride. When my thoughts were not of Eve, I have considered her. When I made my demands of my father, when I played the monster and made my threats, I had thought having a companion of my own kind to be a good and desirable thing. "It is not good for man to be alone," the Lord God is supposed to have said. And so he created a helpmate for Adam, a companion, a lover.

What did that first Eve think when she opened her eyes and found herself joined to Adam, at first figuratively and then physically? Did she accept the role that had been given her, or did she resent it and her lack of choice? Was her sin one of disobedience or of rebellion? And when she and Adam were cast out, did she look at the other tribes of men in search of something that, if not better, was different? Something she chose, something not forced on her.

My Eve chose. Chose to leave her Adam for something that if not better was different. The new Eve, the one my father may even now be creating, will not have that choice. She will be pulled from the darkness and brought into the light with a mind less than a child's. She will be given to me to teach and to raise, to mold as I see fit. And even if I do not take advantage of her vulnerability, even if, like the Beast in the story, I wait to make her my wife until she comes to me, the first choice would still have been mine and not hers.

I do not want to be that kind of monster, one who would force choices upon innocents. I pray that when I meet my father that he has not yet succeeded in the task I have given him. If such is the case, I will release him from all promises, embrace him as a son should his father, then maybe take ship to the Americas and new choices. If however, he presents me with a bride, I shall do my best to raise her as I should have been raised and make sure that any choices she makes are hers alone.

63

The bloody scene that Victor had left behind told the authorities a false story, one of a falling out between criminals. The two men, Lee and Conrad, were known procurers and suspected resurrectionists. The young boy was evidence as to what the teacher had wanted to purchase. A dispute over the boy's price or resistance on the part of the would-be victim, with gunfire and knife play following. The weapons found on the scene told the mostly inexperienced constables a false story. No one then knew about the girl. Her family had not yet reported her missing.

So as Victor traveled north, he was pursued only by the fear of being caught and his own conscience. The later was too weak to force him to change his course and its objections were barely whispers in his mind.

Victor had originally thought to travel to the Orkney Islands whose isolation would be perfect for the monstrous task ahead of him. Instead, he stopped in the Cairngorm Mountains after finding a vacant lodge near the River Tilt.

The woman was by now several days dead, far past the time where the elixir could have restored her to herself. Placing her body in the back room, Victor stripped her of her clothing, made notes of her condition, and gave her the injection.

As with the body of Fritz, the elixir was slow to work. After two hours, Victor injected the woman again. After another two hours, her skin yellowed and her lips turned black. Rather than being repulsed as he was the first time, Victor took this as a sign of progress. One more injection and he retired for the evening.

When he awoke, he observed by the morning light shining through a window the steady rising and falling of her chest. Placing his listening tube to her, he heard the beating of her heart. She was alive, yet not alive. Now all he needed was a storm.

It was only after the elixir had done its work and healed her death wound, that Victor began to see not the corpse of the girl that he had allowed to die but the body of an attractive young woman. Her firm breasts, her full hips, her shapely limbs, her red hair both above and below. She was to him beautiful, a different beauty than the body of Anna Felder, or the restored Justine, who had offered herself to him in gratitude, or the way he pictured Elizabeth would be when she revealed herself to him. No, this young woman had her own beauty and when he looked upon it, Victor felt desire grow.

No, he told himself, *she is not mine*. She was his creation, an innocent to be newly born into this world. She was promised to the monster. It was with some effort that he tore himself away from her. Covering her naked form, he retired to the front room to make his journal entries.

He tried to stay away from her. He took walks and explored along the riverside, making notes of what he found. Sitting outside the lodge, he tried to write a much-delayed letter to Elizabeth. He wrote of wedding plans and alluded subtly to their wedding night. But when he did so, his mind turned to the young woman in the back room of the lodge, one whose naked form was hidden only by a sheet.

Continuing with his letter, he wrote of soon meeting Henry in Belfast and of their journey home. He asked her to tell his father and brother of how he missed them as well and how he hoped they were well. He promised that on his return they would set a wedding date after which they would retire from the world at Lake Como where they would be truly united.

But his words were only that – words. There was no meaning in them, not for Victor. He wrote what was expected of him while the thought, the passion he should have put into his writing were instead in his mind and his mind was in the back room. Somehow he finished and sealed the letter to be posted in Glasgow before he took ship for Belfast.

This chore done, Victor slowly made his way to where the monster's bride lay. Removing her covering, he again examined her. All was well, her body was still warm and breathing. Then, almost as if it were acting on its own, his hand reached out and touched her breast. It was a touch both soft and quick, Victor pulling his hand back as if the electricity was already flowing through her body. For a moment, he felt shame but then he touched her again. This touch was as soft but not quick and any sense of shame fled from him as his hands explored her entire body. He told himself that this was probably nothing new to the woman, that back in Perth she must have allowed men to touch her so, either for pleasure or profit.

Even as his body responded to his touching of her, so did hers. Again, there was the arousal he had felt earlier in the day, that he had felt on seeing Anna Felder and Justine Moritz. But this time there was not the presence of Augustus Darvell or Henry Clerval to restrain him. His love for Elizabeth and his resolve to remain pure until their wedding forgotten, he told himself that this woman before him was unaware and not fully alive and had no doubt had carnal knowledge of men before her death. With that thought, he undressed and climbed on to the table where she lay.

What have I done? Victor asked himself sometime after he had finished his assault on the woman. She had been untouched by man. He felt guilt, guilt over what he had done to her, guilt over his betrayal of Elizabeth and the creature. Mostly he felt guilt at his own weakness. A voice whispered that only a monster could commit such a heinous act. Oddly, the other voice not only agreed but demanded he embrace his darkness, to plunge headfirst into the abyss. Again, ignoring them as best as he was able, Victor vowed not to sin again, that the next time he entered the back room would be to prepare her – no, not *her* but *the body*, for the storm.

Even as his lips spoke the words it was, he knew, was a false vow, like the one he had made to remain true to Elizabeth. He knew that having tasted forbidden fruit he could not resist its sweet delight again and he hated himself for it. But no, this was not his fault. Not truly. Deep in Victor's breast he felt a silent fury rise and burn within him. Victor hated her, this unnamed woman whose body had led him to this. He hated her for being caught and he hated her for being killed. He hated Gaffner, Lee, and Conrad for their part in bringing him to this point. Most of all, he hated the monster who, by his threats to his loved one, had driven him to this.

And now I am about to create another one. No doubt the creature will slake his lust upon her body as I did. They will mate, and mate again until they begin to produce children like themselves, the start of a new race of beings that being stronger and faster than mankind, will one day supplant us.

The scientist in him told him that it was equally likely that the creatures would be sterile, condemned to be the only ones of their kind. Or they might produce human children. But fear overrode reason. He thought of the axe that lay in the wagon.

I should end this now. Take the axe and end her while she is not yet fully alive. Then await the monster and end him. And if that means my own end it is no more than I deserve for creating him.

But his resolve quickly gave way to primitive passion and he knew that he could not destroy such beauty, not yet anyway. And he knew that he would be returning to the back room again and again, at least until the storm.

64

By chance, Adam Frankenstein's ship landed him in Edinburgh. He had no guide, no idea where his father might be, but he had the means by which to find him. When he was on Mont Blanc, he was guided to his father by the link between them. Like calls to like and they were bonded by the elixir that ran through both their veins. Adam had felt it earlier, when he injected then buried the false priest. And then there was the other, the girl Henry had said they had revived and sent to Lake Como. He had sensed her one night, a faint calling of her spirit to his. Whether she was aware of their bond he did not know, but on certain nights he felt her and was able to track her movements, from Lake Como and then east. Soon he lost all trace of her. He hoped it due to distance and nothing else.

And so away from the city, in the quiet of a country night, he emptied his mind of all thought and searched for his father. An hour, then two, then three went by. Finally, just before dawn, he felt the lightest touch, a light tug that seemed to be pulling him north. He set out the next morning by foot, living off the land, avoiding towns and people. It was safer that way. His size, appearance, the fact that he was a stranger who knew little of the local languages meant that he was automatically suspect and a convenient scapegoat in the resolving of any trouble he might come upon.

As Adam moved north, past Falkirk, Stirling, Blackford, and Dunning, he was at first drawn towards the city of Perth. As he approached it, his sense of Victor grew stronger.

Can you feel me, Father? I am coming and one way or the other there will be a reckoning.

But two days out of the city the pull grew weaker. He thought to enter the town and ask questions. He would say that he was the servant of the great Doctor Frankenstein and had been separated from his master. At the least, he would rest at a tavern for one night and sleep on a soft bed rather than the cold ground. But as he neared the town he heard the sound of men coming and hid. As they passed, he heard them speak of a horrible murder in which three men and one boy were killed.

"And now they're saying that a girl is missing,"

"So what, girls go missing all the time."

"This one was seen with the boy. Maybe there was someone else."

"If there was they're both long gone. Bad business all around."

Oh, Father, what have you done? And am I the cause of it?

And so Adam gave up the soft bed, avoided Perth, and followed the elixir's pull further north.

Sometime later, Adam entered the great forest known as the Cairngorms. *I am close, very close,* he told himself. *It is time to finish this.*

Late that morning the sky began to darken, and it was clear that by evening there would be a storm, a storm which he knew from experience would cause his body to tingle every time the sky lit up. To him, the thunder was like a mother calling to her child and the lighting was as if she was feeding him. After every storm, he felt newly enervated as if he had been reborn. Adam had wondered what might happen if, during such a tempest, he held a metal rod in his hand and offered it to the storm. Would his mother reach down to embrace him, and if so, would she make him stronger? Or would she take back what she had given him and leave him a lifeless husk?

One day I might try it, he thought as from his shelter he watched the clouds roll in and heard faint traces of his mother's voice. *And I believe that I would welcome either outcome.*

Someday, but not that day, for he knew that, with his father close, the storm also presaged the possible birth of a being like himself – a companion, a sister, possibly a mate and lover. She would need him and, although he had left his heart in Geneva, he would not abandon her as his father had abandoned him.

65

The boats from the *Rover* delivered its cargo to the shore where it was received by the Night Riders. Watching through a glass aboard his ship, Henry studied their leader. The Moon was slim that night, not quite a smugglers' moon but close enough, and bright enough so that Henry could see that the man Captain Collyer called "Scarecrow." Seemingly a tall man, he sat astride a black horse. The rags in which he was dressed explained his name. His face was covered as were the faces of those to whom he gave orders. MacTire did not seem to be among them, which suited Henry fine. If he never saw the bestial MacTire again, it would be too soon.

As Henry watched, a shout came over the water from the land. "Halt in the King's name!" There were flashes of fire and the delayed sounds of gunfire as British troops charged. Then over all the Scarecrow could be heard to out, "We are betrayed, but so are you."

Night Riders who had been in concealment rose up behind the soldiers even as those on the beach emptied their own pistols. As the soldiers fell, the Scarecrow's cackling laughter wafted toward the ship. Making no effort to help the fallen soldiers, the Night Riders carried away their dead and injured comrades along with their smuggled goods. As they faded into the darkness, there was more laughter as the Scarecrow turned his black horse and rode off into the night.

Watching from the deck of the Rover, Henry's First Mate said to him, "I hope whoever sold them out got a good price. And I pray that he never lives to spend it."

"From the looks of things, it appears that both sides were betrayed," Henry said.

"Traitors everywhere, on both sides," the mate replied. "It's odd that the soldiers waited until we were away. Don't you think, Captain?"

To this Henry had nothing to say except, "I suppose it's good that this was our last trip."

"Yours at least, Captain."

From the way the mate said it, Henry was not certain if this was a threat or not.

"

Standing outside the old lodge, Victor found himself thinking of home. Once again, he stood on the balcony of his room and watched the storm come in. In the distance, he saw the lightning and heard the thunder.

Soon. Soon the storm would come.

He was ready. The Franklin rod was on the roof. The cables joined it to the metal netting that encased the restrained girl. All was ready for the storm.

Soon. Soon he would call down the lightning and, like God, bring the spark of life to the girl.

Soon she would be born anew. Soon he would lose her. This woman whom he had used to pleasure himself.

Another flash. The thunder answering more quickly now. A half an hour, maybe less. He should get ready.

Then he felt – something else. Something calling to him, something that drew him to it. He had felt something like it when he was reviving Justine, and again as he ascended Mont Blanc. Suddenly he realized that he had been feeling the call for some days now and with the realization knew what it was.

The elixir, it was calling to him. *The monster*, he thought, then decided, *No. I am not where he would search. I am safe from him. The girl. It is the elixir in the girl that calls me. That would explain … what I have done. It truly was not my fault. Not the fault of anyone then. She called and I responded. I am not to blame. But what of after she revives. Will the call be stronger? What then? She will be like a child, but can I resist? I must, I …*

Another flash, the thunder almost on top of it. All other thoughts fled as Victor ran to the back room.

The storm was upon them, the rain battering the roof, the wind shaking the building. Lighting and thunder came as one. As before, the body on the table convulsed as power from the heavens raced down the cable.

Victor let the lightning have its way with the woman. Once, twice, a third, then a fourth time her body arching as it ran through her.

The storm passed. Victor waited until its noise had faded away before removing the netting. Leaving her straps in place he examined her.

She was still breathing, her heart still beat. As before, her eyes remained shut and there was no other movement.

Victor had expected this and so waited and watched. It was not her hands that moved first but her feet, moving back and forth. Her legs strained against the straps, then her arms did likewise.

A moaning from her throat. *Soon*, Victor thought, and as he bent low, the young woman opened her eyes and stared into the face of her creator.

And screamed.

Slowly Adam moved through the storm. It was a struggle. His clothes were soddened and weighed heavily on him. He had to pull his shoes from the mud only to have them sink deep again with each step. But the pull of the elixir spurred him on and the lighting gave him strength and so with each step he moved closer to his goal. Soon he saw the lights of a distant building.

The sky brightened just as his mother called to him. Looking at the building, he saw lightning play around a metal rod on the roof. It struck, and struck again, and again. As it did, the pull of the elixir inside him grew stronger and stronger still. This was no faint trace of his father that he had been following. No, it was the calling of one birthed by lightning to another. It was the cry of his sister, his companion, possibly one day his lover, being born.

Adam's heart rejoiced. *One of my own kind*, he thought. *How could I have thought to ask my father not to create her? I must go to her, and I pray that God hears the prayers of one such as I, or rather, hears the prayers of creatures like us, that she will feel towards me as I already feel towards her.*

In a mind still forming, some memory remained. There was a life as a daughter, a sister, and a woman who had already picked the man she would one day marry.

There were the men who grabbed her, who bound her, who killed her. When she again opened her eyes (where had she been?) the sight of one of these men awakened her memories. She sensed that he had not only killed her but had done other things as well. He had used and degraded her. And now she was again bound, still at his mercy.

And so she screamed.

Looking down at his new creation, Victor saw madness in her eyes. She would not stop screaming. *Why?* he asked. This did not happen with the monster, nor with Justine. Why?

He looked again. The madness was still there. Putting his hands on her shoulders, he tried to calm her. She only raised her head as best she could and tried to bite him. No, not bite, she snarled and her teeth snapped as if she wanted to rip the skin from his bones.

Why? he asked again. *I did nothing different.* Then he realized that he had. He had given her the Elixir of Life but in using her as he did, he had also put into her another life-giving fluid. *Could this be the cause? Could the essence I have spilled into her somehow awakened her, changed her, driven her to madness? Will it pass. Or must I …*

Giving out a loud cry, the woman on the table strained against her bonds. Fearful of the strength and vitality the elixir had given her, Victor did not want to wait to see if her fit passed. Nor did he wish to confront this maddened creature should she free herself.

He ran for the axe that lay in the front room.

Approaching the lodge, Adam heard a woman screaming. Not knowing what was happening, he hoped the reason was akin to an infant's cry when it is first born. He tried to hurry but the aftermath of the storm – mud, downed tree limbs – slowed his progress. As he moved closer and closer he felt the connection that he had with the new creation begin to fade. It was gone by the time he reached and opened the door.

Seeing no one in the front room. Adam ran into the back.

There he beheld a horrific sight.

His father standing over a bound woman, his arms raised, an axe in his hands. Adam rushed toward him but was too late. There had already been several blows to the body and head, this was the last. The bloody blade bit deeply into the woman's throat and her severed head fell to the floor.

With a bestial cry, he grabbed the axe from Victor's hand and threw it across the room. Then he did the same to his father. Landing near the axe, Victor started to reach for it.

"Go ahead, Father. I would welcome death, either mine or yours." Victor eased away from the axe. "No? What is it, Father? Have you only courage enough to destroy a helpless woman? Then the death will have to be yours."

Adam's vision went rosy red. As he approached him, Victor remained on the floor. "Here, Father, I prove myself the monster you believe me to be. I will slowly break your limbs, one by one, your legs, your arms, all broken in many places. And then I will leave you, knowing that the elixir flowing however weakly through your veins will keep you alive and suffering. Or maybe I will not simply leave you but do as I once did before, bury you deeply so that you spend whatever life the elixir gives you in the cold, dark ground."

There was a foul odor as Victor's bowels and bladder gave way. Then came his piteous cry, "Please."

"Please what, Father?" Adam pointed to the headless corpse on the table. "Please show you the mercy you failed to show her. Please grant you the kindness you failed to give me." Victor's only reply was sobbing. "So be it, then."

Adam slowly moved closer, deliberately prolonging the moment. *I should kill him*, he thought, *rip his head from his body and leave him here with his crimes. Then go and claim Elizabeth as mine. But she still would not have me. Love me as she says she does, she would wait for Victor until there was no hope left. What then? Would she marry Ernest just to claim the title Frankenstein? No, she may love me but she would never marry a monster like me.*

Then Adam Frankenstein remembered that once he had prayed to never again have to choose to be a monster. That this prayer had not been answered was evident by his standing over his father and deciding his fate.

"Well, do what you must," an angry Victor said through his tears as he demanded his fate. "Prove yourself a monster."

I am only a monster by my choice. And I chose not to be one. I chose not to be my father.

"One like you, Father. I think not." Adam stepped away. "Go, leave here before I change my mind. You are safe – for now. But know this, Father. I will be with you on your wedding night and one day I may yet take from you your bride as you have taken mine."

Gathering what he could, Victor fled the house. Adam watched his father flee. After Victor's cart was out of sight he buried the remains of the young woman and set off on his own journey home.

67

From the journal of Victor Frankenstein.

After too many days' travel, I am finally en route to Belfast where I hope to meet with Henry and escape these cursed isles. Even so, there is a part of me that thinks it best to remain, to return to Cambridge and spend my days in secluded study. How else might I protect Elizabeth?

"I will be with you on your wedding night." Such was his threat. How can I wed if from my wedding comes tragedy? Yet how can I not? I have given Elizabeth my word that on my return we shall be married. She will hold me to it, unless I tell her the truth, that I created and abandoned life, that I have killed, that I allowed a young woman to die, that I revived this woman only to ravish her over and over then kill her again. That I have become every bit a monster as the one I've created.

I cannot. I cannot make the confession I should, for all will think me mad and shut me away. Perhaps that would be for the best and I would allow it if it were not for that damned creature.

There can be no peace for me, for Elizabeth, for my family as long as that monster lives.

"I will be with you on your wedding night." I have no doubt that he will and so that is when I must end him. I will marry Elizabeth, and I will make her bridal chamber my fortress. With gun and blade, I will defend her and if I fall it will be worth the sacrifice if only I can take him with me. It is said that the eyes are the windows of the soul. Perhaps, but they are also the window to the brain. Shots fired into the eyes may pierce the brain and kill it.

That is what I must do. I created this foul thing and on my wedding night I will destroy it, whatever the cost to me.

There is a cry from above. Belfast is sighted.

❦❦

Henry never knew who decided that he should die. Was it the United Irishmen, who once his usefulness to them ended decided that would everyone save him would be better off? Or did they suspect that he had been working with Captain Collyer and so killed him as an informer? Or was it Collyer or one of his men who made the decision? Or maybe it was the Scarecrow exacting punishment for the ambush Henry had helped set up?

He did know who killed him. It was the beautiful, redhaired young lady who had once come to his door and handed him a note. When the knock came and he opened the door there she was. When he saw her, Henry expected another note. What he did not expect was a whispered "Sorry."

And she stepped aside to allow three men to enter his rooms. One man held him while the other two beat him unmercifully. When he was no longer capable of standing they let him fall and began to kick him.

Henry remained conscious for most of the assault. It was not until he felt a heavy boot alongside his head that his vision blurred. Oddly, his pain began to fade with his eyesight and it was not long after that that he saw and felt nothing more.

69

Dear Father,
Henry Clerval is dead, foully murdered in Belfast. And there is worse news, I am being held for his death.

My sojourn in Scotland did not go well. I was forced to flee that country and seek out Henry in Ireland. When I found him, he lay on the floor, his death obvious.

No sooner had I entered then two men rushed in and declared me Henry's murderer, stating that he had been seen alive just before I ascended to his quarters. This was, of course, a lie. From Henry's condition, it was clear that he had been dead no less than a day and his injuries were such that more than one man had caused them. But Henry and I were both strangers and it was easier for the gardai to blame one foreigner for the death of another than to find the real killers.

On you, Father, I must give the unwelcomed task of letting the Clerval family know of Henry's death. Please extend to them my sympathies and my assurances that despite what they may hear, I am innocent of his murder. Please tell my dear Elizabeth that once I am freed, I will return to her as soon as possible to make her my wife.

Father, I do not know how but I am sure that I will free myself of this baseless charge and will return to House Frankenstein as soon as the Good Lord permits.

From the journal of Victor Frankenstein.
I have written a letter to my father telling him of my plight. While in it I express my hope that I will soon be freed I am afraid that without outside help the case against me will go as poorly as did the case against Justine Moritz did against her. Although in my case there will no one to revive me once the hangman's noose snaps my neck.

But I may not need reviving and that thought frightens me more than does my death. Thanks to Henry, the elixir of life flows through my veins. Because of it, I may live on even after my hanging. If that is the case, I fear that the next step in this superstitious country where they see fairies and "wee folk" everywhere will be to burn me as a witch, subjecting me to the extreme agony of the flames through which I still may survive. Maybe if I am convicted, when I am convicted, I can ask the mercy of a simple beheading. That would be fitting, given my treatment of the poor woman whom I assaulted and twice killed.

The irony is that I have the perfect defense but it is one that I cannot use. I had my bags with me when I went to Henry's rooms. Between the time I found his body and the men rushed in I was able to inject him with the elixir. But his body was removed and buried before it could take effect. He is right now in a grave. If only I could have him exhumed, I could show that his lungs are breathing and his heart beating and that there are no signs of violence on his person.

I have asked that this be done but have been mocked and derided as an impious sinner whose request shows the blackness of his heart.

Of course, I know who Henry's real killer is. It is the monster, the thing who once vowed to take those whom I love from me. Somehow he knew my plans and, going ahead of me, found and killed Henry. Despite what I wrote in the letter to my father, one man could have caused Henry's wounds, if that one man were a monster.

I have been given an advocate, a Mr. Kirwin. He is most interested in my case and believes that I may have a chance, a "slim chance" as he put it, of acquittal. When I suggested that poor Henry's body night not show the signs of assault described by my accusers he stated that after so many days it might not be possible to tell. Nevertheless, he stated that he would suggest it, on the principle that when confronted with his killer, a murdered man would rise up in accusation.

"Not that you or I believe such nonsense, but most of these people do. Nevertheless, it is an excuse to exhume the body."

How close Kirwan was to the truth he would never know. One storm, one lucky lightning strike, and Henry would rise up. But that was not to be.

When the gardai went to Henry's grave they found that it had already been opened and that his body was missing. They are at a loss to explain this, but I know the truth.

It was the creature who haunts me. It was he who stole Henry's body so as to deny me my defense. Now there is no proof that I did not kill him, although Mr. Kirwan states that he will argue that without an available corpus delicti *to present (in theory) in court there is no proof of murder or even death.*

It a tiny candle of hope flickering in a vast darkness. Now all I can do is to await whatever fate might bring, and pray for the soul of Henry Clerval, whose spirit I have may trapped between life and heaven.

70

When Henry Clerval opened his eyes, it took a moment before they adjusted to the brightness of the room. When he could again see clearly, he was greeted by the sight of Adam Frankenstein smiling down at him.

Henry's last memories were of being beaten to death. Finding himself alive … he knew it was possible, but he wasn't sure how it had been accomplished. There were other questions as well.

"It has been three months since you died," the large man said softly. "Welcome back."

"How, where …"

"You are in an unused hunting lodge in the Cairngorm Mountains of Scotland. It was here that Victor Frankenstein murdered the woman who was to be my wife. It was here that I almost killed him, and here where I decided that, unlike my father, I would not be a monster. As for how, once my father fled his crime and my presence, I followed him after burying his victim. I was a day behind him. As best as I can piece things together, on finding your lifeless body, he managed to inject it with the elixir just before he was arrested for your murder. I waited until after you were buried, stole your body, and returned here. Using the equipment abandoned by my father, I revived you."

"But Victor, he is innocent."

"Yes, I know," Adam said, "Or else why did he give you the elixir?"

"But I must save him, I must go back."

"And say what?" Adam asked laughingly. "That you were dead but are now alive. Other than you, me, sweet Justine, and my poor bride, the last time that happened was in the Bible. Were you to appear and if they believed you, both you and he would probably be burned as demons or witches. And I will not have the time and trouble it took me transporting your body from Belfast to here wasted. No, leave my father where he is."

"But he is innocent."

"It is fitting punishment for the crimes he has already committed," Adam said harshly, then waved his hand. "But do not worry, my friend. Before I was able to find a ship that would take us across the Irish Sea, I heard that Victor's father Alphonse was on his way to Ireland. He is a rich man and I have no doubt that he and those holding his son will come to an arrangement. After all, who cares what one foreigner does to another when there is gold to be had. Victor will be freed and father and son will return to Geneva where Victor and Elizabeth will be wed."

"And what of you, my friend?"

"I too will travel to Geneva. I promised my father that I would be with him on his wedding night.

Up until now, Henry had been lying in bed, his body raised up on one arm. Now he started to rise, intent on confronting the other man.

"If you mean harm to Victor or Elizabeth remember our discussion on how you may be killed."

Adam nodded, "I remember, and with the elixir in your veins it would be an interesting struggle. But I mean no harm to Elizabeth, and the next time I raise a hand to my father will be the last. And I want him to live a long life, for whenever he thinks himself safe from me, whenever he believes that I have forgotten him, then I will reveal myself to him. As I said, he may lead a long life but it will not be a peaceful or happy one. On his wedding night, he will see me. Perhaps he will know what I have done, perhaps not.

"As for you, my friend, I am afraid that Henry Clerval is dead and you must seek a new life. What will you do?"

Henry thought for a moment. "I will miss my life but death has given me a new one and I will make the most of it. I enjoyed my time aboard the *Star Tender*. Perhaps I will go to sea, maybe join an expedition to the polar north."

Adam held out his hand. "We are now brothers of a sort and I wish you well. Wherever you roam and whatever you do, may God and Fate be kind to you. Remain here as long as you like. I must return to Geneva. There is a wedding I must attend."

71

My dearest Elizabeth,

I am happy to tell you that, thanks to the efforts of my father and Mister Kirwan, all charges against me in Henry's unfortunate death have been dismissed. With the financial backing of my father, Mister Kirwan launched a new investigation of Henry's death. Mister Kirwan found witnesses willing to swear that Henry was threatened by those who wanted him to use the ship he had acquired for illegal purposes. Also, the doctor who examined Henry's body was convinced to reexamine his notes and upon further review stated that Henry may have been killed the day before my arrival. As Henry's body had been stolen just after his burial, there was no way to determine the true time of Henry's death.

Given this evidence, or rather the lack of evidence of death and any motive I had for killing a man who had been a life-long friend and almost a brother to me, my father and Mister Kirwan convinced the authorities to release me into my father's custody on condition that I quit Ireland and vow never to return.

So I am fulfilling my vow to return home. After my father and I cross the Channel, we are taking a coach that will bring us back to Geneva and me back to you. Our long-delayed nuptials shall take place as soon as possible after I set foot in my own home, never to stray far from it again. Instead, I look forward to spending the rest of my life with you, managing the estate for my father, and raising children so that House Frankenstein will continue for generations to come.

And speaking of raising children, I hope that you will not think me too bold if I confess that as much as I look forward to our wedding, I also look forward to the night that will follow it, a night on which our bodies and souls will unite as one. I long for that night, a night too long delayed when in shared joy we give to each other the gift that can be given only once. Until that night, as I lay in my lonely bed, my thoughts and my dreams will be only of you.

With all my love,
Victor

Victor sent the letter days before the departure of his father and him. It would arrive in Geneva about a week before they did. Even as he sealed the letter, he thought about the lies he had told in it and realized that he cared little about telling them.

Yes, he did look forward to bedding Elizabeth, on receiving the bridal gift of her maidenhead. That he had "given his gift" to a barely alive woman whose name he had never learned bothered him not. As for the "investigation", there was none. His father had money, Kirwan and those to whom he had spoken wanted it. Henry's missing body and Victor's lack of motive was not a concern. He could have murdered Henry in full view of a dozen people and the result would have been the same.

"Science and knowledge are wonderful things, Victor," his father told him just after he was released from custody. "But it is business that rules the world. It was business that obtained your release, just as it was probably an ill-conceived business in which Henry was involved that got him killed, or so a captain of the gardai suggested to me. Now we will say no more about this. On our return to Geneva, you will marry your cousin, begin to work at my side, and learn what it is to be a man of House Frankenstein, rather than a boy playing at fancies."

Father, Victor wrote in his journal, *if you only knew what those fancies of mine have led to. On my wedding night, I will take my joy of my bride as if my right. But I will also be watchful of the creature who had threatened her life and my happiness. She will be the bait that lures the creature to its doom. And if that doom requires the death of my cousin, so be it. I can always marry again.*

72

The long-anticipated marriage between Victor Frankenstein, scion of the House Frankenstein and Elizabeth Lavenza, was not the elaborate affair that had been planned since it was decided that those two should wed.

There were rumors surrounding Henry's death – that Victor killed him while rejecting Henry's advances, that Victor killed him during a lovers' quarrel, that it was a business arrangement between the men gone sour, that Victor escaped punishment due to his father's money. A scandal involving Victor and a murdered college professor accused of graverobbing was revived and given new life. There were threats made by Henry's family that they would seek their own justice.

Because of this, it was decided to hold a small, private wedding – family and those friends who remained loyal to the Frankensteins only. Supposedly because of the threats, Victor began to go armed, openly carrying pistols and knives to defend his life and those of his family. Victor had his own reasons for bearing arms but the threats made by the Clervals were a good excuse to practice and improve his marksmanship until he could strike a small target at a reasonable distance.

Should the Clervals attack, so be it, he wrote, *but I'd rather put a ball through the eye and into the brain of the monster. Let him appear on my wedding night. It will be the last I see of him in this world.*

As the wedding day approached, both the bride and groom became increasingly more nervous. Friends and family attributed this to the couple's upcoming wedding day, and wedding night. And in part they were correct, but the real reasons were the secrets they kept hidden in their hearts and souls, secrets about the one Victor had called "monster" and "creature" and Elizabeth had called "Adam" and "my Beast" and "beloved." Both wondered where he was, and both watched and worried that he would appear as had Banquo at the feast.

But the day came at last. Storms threatened but held off as if in honor of the occasion. As Victor stood with his brother Ernest and Elizabeth walked down the aisle on the arm of her uncle to the strains of Pachelbel's *Canon and Gigue in D*, there had been no sightings of the one they feared.

After the now joined couple celebrated with friends and relations, after the jests and toasts, they left in a carriage for a villa outside the city, one close to the Frankenstein estate.

Night came. The servants discreetly withdrew to the other side of the villa. In separate rooms, Elizabeth and Victor prepared themselves for each other.

The storm that had passed over the wedding now struck. Rain beat down upon the house and in the distance thunder could be heard.

In the bridal chamber, Victor stood at the window and watched the storm. *Where are you?* he asked the monster he knew had to be out there. *You were born in a storm. How fitting that you shall die in one.*

Against the creature's threat, he had already secreted pistols and knives throughout the chamber so that whenever and wherever his nemesis struck he would be prepared.

As Victor watched and wondered, from behind him he heard,

"Victor, husband, are you coming to bed?"

He turned to see Elizabeth, his cousin, his wife, and soon to his lover, standing by the bed. The gown she wore was mostly transparent and he could easily make out the curves of her hips, the shape of her breasts, the dark circles that were her nipples, and the light patch between her legs. She got into bed and under the blankets. One swift movement later, the gown flew from beneath the covers and on to the floor.

Victor felt his excitement grow. Slowly he removed his clothes and joined his wife in bed.

Had the couple's meal lasted slightly longer, had Elizabeth taken more time in preparing herself for her marriage bed, had Victor lingered longer at the window, he would have seen revealed by the lightning a figure almost seven-foot tall staring at the ground level window behind which were Victor Frankenstein and his bride.

Adam had tried to stay away. He had told himself that all would be better off if he were somewhere else – England, the Palestine, the Americas. But something drew him to Geneva. And as the storm raged around him, he tortured himself with the thought of the man he had cause to hate being with the woman he could not help but love. He thought of the times he and his Eve had joined their bodies, of the carnal passion shared by the beast and his beauty, and his heart broke and his soul shattered in such a way that not even if he injected himself with the one remaining vial of elixir he had carried away from Scotland, the pain would not go away.

In bed with Elizabeth, Victor embraced his bride. His hands caressed her body, his lips tasted her breasts, his fingers found and probed her feminine secret. Soon,

"I am ready, Victor."

He covered her, she yielded to him, and they became one. But even as Victor heard Elizabeth moan in what seemed to be pain then passion, even as he reached and expressed his own carnal pleasure, the memory of an unknown woman came back to him. There had been resistance the first time he had taken her, proof that she had been untouched. There had been no such resistance with Elizabeth. His mind sought an explanation other than the obvious, and then …

"I shall be with you on your wedding night," had been the monster's threat, but it had been no threat. It had been a mocking claim that his creature had despoiled his bride.

"I may yet take from you your bride as you have taken mine."

The creature had said this knowing that he had already been with Victor's bride. And now Victor lay in bed with a woman who had, willingly or not, taken into her the seed of a foul beast.

"Victor, my love, are you all right?"

He was not. Whatever love he had for her had turned into hate. Springing from the bed, he shouted, "There was someone before me," he shouted in accusation and from the look on her face he knew it was true. "You have lain with him."

Desperately, Elizabeth tried to soothe her husband, but he would not be calmed. "Whore, foul Jezebel!" he shouted.

He has gone mad, she thought but still hoped to calm him, if only enough so that she could get dressed and flee. But then he drew out two pistols from their concealment under a chair cushion and pointed them at her.

That's when she screamed.

Over the sounds of the storm, there came a woman's scream. This was not a cry of passion fulfilled – he had heard such cries from Elizabeth more than once. No, this was a cry of fear and terror.

Adam's mind returned to the night in Scotland when his bride had been birthed and murdered. The scream he had heard then was like the one coming from the villa. This time, though, his footing was solid and he resolved he would not be too late again.

Elizabeth sat up in bed, a sheet covering her body. "Victor, no! I can explain." She could not, but maybe her husband would pause enough to let her escape into the storm.

"I need no lies from you, harlot," Victor shouted as he aimed his pistol.

There was the sound of shattering glass as Adam broke open the outside doors to the bedroom and burst in.

"Adam," Elizabeth cried, letting fall the sheet to reveal her naked form. With her in bed, there was no way for Adam to protect her. Hoping to draw Victor's attention away from Elizabeth, Adam rushed him, shouting, "This ends tonight, Father."

Hurriedly, Victor fired first one pistol then the other, the first shot going wide, the second striking Adam's shoulder. Ignoring his pain, the maddened creature reached for his creator, intent on tearing his father's head from his shoulders so that for him there could be no resurrection.

What stopped Adam and what saved Victor was the latter falling to his knees and crying out in a maddened voice,

"NO!"

Adam turned and saw that the shot that had passed by him had found its target in Elizabeth. The projectile had torn a hole in her left breast and her blood was staining the bed linen.

"You killed her," Adam shouted at his father even as his conscience acknowledged his own part in this tragedy. He still would have killed his father but for the pounding on the bedroom doors and the shouts from outside that threatened to drown out the still raging storm.

The servants of the villa were naturally reluctant to intrude on a wedding night. They knew to ignore cries and shouts. They had heard these noises and more time and again. But they could not ignore pistols shots and screams of terror. While some tried to break through the locked doors of the bedroom, others braved the storm to force an entrance from outside. They did not have to. The outside doors stood open and shattered and in the doorway stood a large man with a hideous face contorted in madness and fury.

Seeing his chance, Victor unlocked the room doors and threw them open. Pointing first at the pistols he had dropped, he cried out, "He killed her. This monster broke in and killed Lady Frankenstein."

Adam found himself beset on both sides. None of his attackers were armed but there were many of them and their number was growing as everyone in the villa was rushing to the room.

Flee, was his first thought. But in doing so he would have to abandon his Eve. But to stay with her meant capture. He knew there would be no trial, that the crowd in its anger would find the weapons needed to tear him to pieces and probably burn his body. Anger and passion took over. Picking up his love's body, he flung it over a shoulder and with one hand fought his way out of the room.

They crowded him, he pushed and shoved them aside. His one advantage was that they seemed loathe to strike Elizabeth, even though they knew her to be dead. More were coming, both behind him and from outside. There was no escape, no hope for the beast or the beauty. He was about to leave her behind, vowing to return for her body whatever the cost, when his vision went red with rage and madness took him.

A primal growl startled his attackers and as they paused he rushed them. He trampled some and broke the necks or backs of others. He fled into the storm and the night, leaving death behind him.

73

As Adam ran, his mind calmed and soon he could again think. He could hear them behind him, but he was faster than they and could see better in the night. Soon their cries and shouts fell away.

Still, they will search, he thought, *if not tonight then in the morning follow. A seven-foot creature carrying a naked woman will not be hard to track, especially with me leaving tracks in earth wet from the storm.*

Or so they believed, he reasoned. The woods were his first home and he could hide in them forever and not be found. But he had Eve with him, and limited time.

Adam found a small clearing. Digging a shallow grave, he placed the body of his love into it then filled it, making sure to spread leaves, branches, and other debris. Once she was as safe and hidden as she could be, he left her there. Listening for the voices of his pursuers he made his way to where he and Eve had once loved. There was something there he needed.

After Victor and Henry had revived Justine in the ruins of the old mansion, they left the Franklin rod in place. It was for this that Adam dared to go there that night. Although there was no possibility that his father would know that this is where he and Elizabeth had rendezvoused but there was a chance that Victor might suspect that he would take shelter there.

Concealed by rain and darkness, Adam retrieved the iron rod from the roof of the mansion. Then he returned to where had buried Elizabeth. The storm had passed. But another one was coming and would be upon them before dawn. *Time enough,* Adam thought. He dug up his love and, carrying her, the iron rod, and some clothing he had found in the mansion, sought high ground.

An hour or two before dawn, Adam waited. But there would be no dawn that day, no Sun, no brightness. Only darkness from the storms. Looking out, he could see lightning flashing in the dark clouds that were coming his way.

Which will find me first, he wondered. *My pursuers or the storm? And when either is upon me, what will happen?*

Some time ago, Adam had wondered what might happen if he offered himself to the storm, if he answered the call of his mother the thunder. Would she reach down to embrace him or would she take back her gift of life? He had thought then that one day he would try it. And now that day had come.

After removing Elizabeth from her grave, Adam had injected her with the last of the Elixir of Life. Now, on the top of the hill, her wound was closing, her chest was rising and falling, and her body was warming.

The rains came and with them thunder and lightning. With one hand he pressed Elizabeth to his side. Holding the iron bar in the other, he held it aloft and waited.

The storm was upon them when his mother answered his call. Thunder and lightning arrived together and struck the iron pole again and again. There was pain like he had never known before as power flowed down the rod, through his body, and into Elizabeth's. He struggled to not only remain standing but, like Moses against the Amalekites, to keep his hand in the air so as to give his love the greatest chance to live again.

Finally, he could stand no longer. He dropped Elizabeth and collapsed, his body falling on top of her, the iron rod rolling away.

74

Evening had fallen by the time Adam awakened. He felt stronger, full of energy. His wound had healed, his flesh having expelled the bullet. Rushing over to Elizabeth, she saw that her wound had healed as well, her breast as perfect as he remembered it. She was breathing normally, as if a babe asleep.

In one respect she was a babe, an infant born into a new life. "May you come to enjoy it," Adam said to his sleeping Eve. He then turned his face to the heavens. The storms having passed, the sky was clear. Looking up, he whispered, "Thank you, Mother." Then he sat and waited for his love to wake.

An hour later, Adam had begun to despair. Henry had not taken this long to revive. But then, Henry had not had to share the current. Finally, a moan. Elizabeth's eyes fluttered, opened, and looked at him.

"Beast, what has happened? Where is Victor? I had a dream …"

"It was no dream, Beauty. You were dead, killed by your husband. I brought you back from the dark abyss."

Elizabeth moaned again as memories flooded her mind. "I remember the church, the priest, my vows and Victor's. We were wed. There was the villa and the bed. I gave myself to Victor as a wife should. But he became enraged and, and … there was you, and there was pain, and then there was blackness, and now there is you again."

Elizabeth looked down and saw that she was naked. She blushed slightly, but she had been naked before Adam many times and so felt little shame.

"I have clothes, ones you left at the ruins, in case, you know."

Another blush. Elizabeth did know. With Adam's help, she stood and dressed.

"I do not understand. Where are we and where is Victor. And did I hear you call him 'Father'?"

"It is a long story, one I will tell you on the way."

"On the way to where?"

"Ingolstadt, or rather, just outside it."

"But why can I not return to Geneva and House Frankenstein."

"It begins with a man who sought to conquer death …"

By the time they reached Ingolstadt and had found the house where the De Laceys had lived, and got settled there, he had told her the whole story – a story of death and resurrection, of deceit and betrayal, and of murder and vengeance. He told her how her cousin William had died and why, how Justine had been brought back just as she had, and that William's killer now lay in the grave meant for Justine. He told her his story and why he had called Victor "Father." He left nothing out save for the true fate of Gerber. He told of his meeting with Victor, the promise he had extracted, and how Victor had first created then destroyed the one who was to be his mate and companion.

"I believe that my father used her carnally before fully reviving her. She must have been untouched at first, which is how he knew that you had not been."

Finally, he told her what he knew of Henry's death, how he had stolen his body, and revived him.

Elizabeth listened to all this and would not have believed it but for her memory of being shot, of the pain of the pistol ball entering her breast, of the blackness and a light that had called to her. That she knew she had been wounded but now bore no scar swayed her to the fact that Adam was telling the truth.

She thought of all that he said, thought of it as they traveled. She said nothing until she and Adam were sitting in the De Lacey's cabin and she was dressed in the clothing of the dead Agatha. She found it somewhat disturbing that the dress she wore fit her and over the food that Adam had obtained from the forest she asked,

"Did you and this … Agatha …?"

"No." Was there regret and sadness in his voice, she wondered. "But had the soldiers not come, I may have stayed and then yes, I would have become part of her family and may never have met my father, never met you. Victor would not have traveled to Britain, Henry would not have been killed, and you would now be the Lady Frankenstein."

Elizabeth thought on this for a moment, then said, "I *am* the Lady Frankenstein, wife of Victor Frankenstein, and I mean to return to Geneva and claim my rightful place."

She said this quietly and with determination, her eyes bright with the passion he had seen only during their lovemaking. He knew that he would not, could not stop her from doing whatever she wanted. But still he said,

"Think, my dear Eve. People other than Victor and me saw your ravaged breast, saw the blood that poured from your wound, heard both Victor and me declare you dead."

"And yet I am alive. Whatever was seen, whatever was heard, the fact is that I am alive."

Adam shook his head. "A dead woman arisen, a dead woman accused by her husband of coming impure to their marriage bed, a dead woman who gave herself to a monster. You can return, I will not stop you, but if you do there will no doubt be a trial, but it will not be Victor who stands accused but you, of carnality and witchery. The former will see you cast out, shamed, and shunned. The latter will see you burned and beheaded. Victor will make sure of that."

For a long time Elizabeth was quietly, tears rolling silently down her cheeks. Then, "Not since sweet William was killed and dear Justine hung for the crime have I felt such misery. I feel like crawling into bed and turning my face to the wall. But from what you tell me, I would lie there forever. Oh, Adam, how I wish you had not called me back from the light in the darkness. Maybe I should return to Geneva and let them do what they will to me."

"Or maybe stay here, at least for as long as we can. If my father is able, he will search for us. He will haunt us as I once haunted him."

"But how will he find us?"

"The elixir inside us. It is our bond. I'm sure you can feel me through it." At her nod, he continued. "Victor has it in him as well. Henry injected him with it to save his life. But he did not die, and so was never christened by the spark. I think his living blood wars with the elixir."

"And where shall we go?" Elizabeth asked bitterly. "How far do we run? To the Ottomans? To India? Shall we lead him to the Northern Wastes and leave his body to be found by a passing ship? No, I do not wish to spend years waiting to be freed only when his frozen body is found. I wish it now, Adam."

"What do you suggest?"

"Let him find us, here. Let it end where it began."

Adam had his doubts, but he knew that to deny her was to lose her. He might lose her anyway, for this cabin was not the estate in which she was raised or which she had longed to possess. But one problem at a time.

"Very well," he said calmly, stifling all worries and misgivings. "It will take planning. For the elixir is strong in us but dim in my father, as we have felt the spark of life and he has not. Still, he will search for us and will one day find us. And when he does, there is no predicting what he might do, for he will come after us with a plan born of anger and madness. But it is late, and it is dark. We should retire for the night."

"And do you expect me to share your bed?"

Adam looked at her, smiled and quoted words that she had once told to him. "The beast was taken by her grace and beauty and fell so in love with her that he did not force himself on her. Rather he waited until the night she came willingly to his bed.

"I will take M. De Lacey's room. You may use Agatha's. Good night, my Beauty."

"Good night, Beast."

They slept apart for three nights. On the fourth, she came willingly to his bed.

75

From the journal of Victor Frankenstein

I am being held in what Magistrate Vernet calls "gentle confinement" until it is decided whether I am a madman or a monster.

After I discovered how Elizabeth has played me false with my own creation, such was my mood that I would have killed her. It would have been my right to punish her for her betrayal rather than quietly put her aside. But I like to think that I would have stayed my hand, listened to her story, and for her sake and my family's forgiven her. It was, I'm sure, not her fault, that he either forced or seduced her. But he was waiting, waiting for me to discover his despoiling of my bride before coming in to mock me. My anger turned towards him and in that anger I fired and missed and so killed her. I may have discharged the pistols but he is the reason she is dead. Again, his actions curse me. All blame lies with the monster.

At first, I placed her death on him. I accused him of breaking in armed, of wanting to kill me and violate her. I made myself the hero, wresting one pistol from him while the other accidentally discharged. He killed my wife and I shot him just before the others broke in.

But M. Vernet is an astute observer, more of a scientist than a magistrate. Talking to those who witnessed the aftermath, he learned of the relative positions of myself, Elizabeth, and the creature (whom for some reason Elizabeth called "Adam"). He noted the powder residue on both my hands. He stood quietly for a time, seemingly doing nothing. But I could see by his eyes he was studying the room. In the end, he nodded and that nod told me that that he knew what had truly occurred as if he had witnessed the events himself.

"Search the room," he said. As his men searched others came in from outside to report that the monster had escaped them.

Looking out on the storm then at the dead men the creature had left behind, he said, "I will not risk any more lives. The search will continue in the morning."

"But that beast has my Elizabeth," I protested.

"She is not yours anymore, Monsieur. She now belongs to God and in part to me. And from what of the servants heard from this room just before the screams and the shots, she never was yours."

I would have struck him then, but there were too many of his men about, and a part of me had to acknowledge that he was correct. She ceased to be mine when the creature possessed her.

"She was my wife," I managed to say but by then Vernet had turned from me towards one of his men.

"Sir," the guardsman said, "we've found four other pistols and three knives."

Vernet turned to me. "Yours, I presume, M. Frankenstein. An odd choice with which to decorate a bridal chamber. I think, Monsieur, that you and I need to speak further."

At his nod two of his men lead me away. I spent the rest of my wedding night in a courthouse cell.

In the morning I was allowed to wash. My brother Ernest brought me fresh clothing.

"How is Father?" I asked him.

"Not well. He collapsed on hearing of Elizbeth's death and your arrest. He has taken to bed and the doctor fears for his life."

"Did he say anything?"

Ernest hesitated and would have said "No" but I insisted.

"Before he lost consciousness, he said, 'I should have left him in Belfast. Then my niece would still be alive'."

I said nothing for I could not disagree.

Once I was dressed and my fast broken with something barely edible, I was led to M. Vernet's office. He bade me sit and offered me chocolate and pastry and we ate and drank in silence as if we were two old friends. When we had finished our paltry feast, he said,

"Now then, M. Frankenstein, I know from an eavesdropping servant that your new wife was not the innocent you expected and that this enraged you. Had you beaten or even killed her that would have been understandable. A crime of passion, your punishment merely a few years.

"But Monsieur, as I said last night, knives and pistols are a strange choice for a wedding night. And the same servant also heard your wife call the intruder 'Adam' and this Adam call you 'Father.' Now then, let us start fresh and you can tell me what truly happened last night. And don't forget to explain the pistols and knives.

I had been hiding my secret for so long, the secret of what I had done and what I had become. Sitting there in Vernet's office, I felt the need to explain and justify my actions.

In the end, I told him everything.

I told him of my journals, of which this is probably the last. They would support my confession. They would tell of Anna Felder, of the deaths of M. Darvell and Fritz, of how and why I came to use Fritz's body to make my monster. They would tell everything, including my violation of the girl and how I let her die the first time. And they told how I was driven to these actions by the menace of the thing I created, the monster who called me "Father." Sadly, where the fault falls may not be as obvious to them as it is to me.

It took two days for me to relate my confession, with Vernet taking notes in a shorthand of his own devising. It took another several days for Vernet to obtain and look over my journals. During this time I was held in a small apartment within the courthouse. "It is for 'special guests,' Vernet explained. It was more comfortable than the cell but anything that locks only from the outside is still a cell.

During my confinement, my father died. He mentioned my name before his end but only to curse it. I was allowed to attend his funeral under guard but was turned away from the church door by my brother who was supported by the Clerval family.

As I sat in Vernet's "gentle confinement" I did not ponder my fate. Death by beheading or immolation no doubt as I had told Vernet that hanging me would probably not be effective. I knew that the monster, my monster, had escaped and I wondered what he had done with Elizabeth's body. What pained me and what will continue to pain me until they light the fire or drop the axe is that had he left her behind I could have brought her back. I had the knowledge and could have bargained for the means. Then both she and my father would still be alive. Two more deaths to lay at my creature's door.

It was ten days after the death of Elizabeth that guards again led me to Vernet's office. Again we had chocolate and pastry. Then he pronounced sentence.

"There will be no trial, Victor. For if there were one, what is contained in your journals would become public. For the good of the Geneva, for the good of the world, I cannot allow that. What you have discovered, what you have done, is both brilliant, monstrous, and an offense against God. Your journals, including the one you will finish tonight, will be confiscated and safely stored in tunnels under the Alps where they will be guarded against the day when they may be needed."

"Who guards them?" I asked.

"Dragons," he replied with no hint of amusement crossing his face.

I let that pass. "What will happen to me?" I was expecting and would have accepted a quiet execution and an unmarked grave. So I was shocked when Vernet said,

"This man Adam will be held responsible for the deaths of Elizabeth Frankenstein née Lavenza and the men he actually killed. If he is caught, well, thanks to you I know how to kill him. The story is that he was a madman who broke into your room thinking you were his father against whom he had an insane hatred. Your wife's cry of 'a man' was misheard as 'Adam.' As for you, you will be released. Your brother, as newly appointed master of House Frankenstein, was provided with a summary of your statement. He has, of course, disowned you but has allowed you enough money for new clothing and the means to leave Geneva. He states that he cannot guarantee your safety should you remain here. Frankly, Victor, neither can I."

With that he had me led back to my room. Tonight I sit, finishing this last entry in my journal. Tomorrow I leave Geneva and the world I know in disgrace.

Before I left his office, Vernet asked me. "What will you do?"

Just then I had no answer. After some thought, I do now. I will track the monster. And should he escape me, I will haunt him as he has haunted me. And when I find him, either I will kill him or him me. Either way, I will find some kind of peace.

And so I end this record of my life. May you who read it think kindly of me.

I wonder if there really are dragons.

Victor, formerly of the House Frankenstein.

76

There are no secrets. What one man seeks to hide another may reveal. Victor knew this. Gradually, the story of Frankenstein and his monster would come out. M. Vernet's shorthand notes would be found by someone who could read them. Or someone who had listened at a door, either in Vernet's office or when the magistrate made his report to his brother Ernest, would tell what he had heard. The story would come out and would grow in the telling.

Then Victor would be as Cain, unwelcomed in any land and shunned by all who saw and knew him. But he would bear no mark of protection and every hand would be against him. Vernet's mercy was no blessing. Better the axe or flame than to become the eternal wanderer.

As he slowly trudged away from Geneva, with everything he owned in a pack or on his belt, with everything he was behind him, and all he had done buried in a cave and guarded by a myth (maybe), Victor looked ahead to a very long, very bleak future.

So many sins have I committed, he thought. *Yet I cannot say I regretted any of them. What I have done, all that I have done, I was driven to do by my nature and desires. Perhaps Calvin was right, and from the moment we are born we are set on a path from which there is no turning. Yet the choices I made seemed like mine. It does not matter*, he finally decided. *There is only one end to this road I am on, and the sooner I come to it the better for all. A quiet place, a sharpened blade, an open vein, and my life's blood draining out of me along with the elixir. Only then might I find peace.*

But no sooner had Victor decided this then he realized that there was still one more thing he had to do. He had vowed to destroy the thing he had created, the monster who was to blame for all the sins he had committed. The creature must be found and killed, only then might there be some redemption for him at the end.

But where to start? To what place might the monster have fled?

He decided to spend his first night of exile in the old ruins in which he had revived Justine. But one he arrived there he found signs of other inhabitants. There were blankets arranged as bedding and one or two items left behind. One of these was a broach. Its catch broken, it had fallen to the ground and had been either abandoned or forgotten.

At once he knew it as Elizabeth's, for he had given it to her.

He knew then that this was where they had met; where the woman meant for him, the woman who as a girl was given to him by his mother, had given herself to that foul creature. As he pictured her with the monster, his body atop her as they coupled, he was glad then that he had killed her for by her actions she had polluted not just herself but him as well by letting him into her body.

Did he flee here that night? If not, where would he have gone? To Scotland? To Mont Blanc? In thinking of Mount Blanc, Victor recalled his conversation there with the thing that dared to call him "Father." The creature had spoken of taking refuge in the forest outside Ingolstadt. That was the beast's first home, and that was where Victor would begin his search.

77

Victor Frankenstein walked the streets of Ingolstadt by night, not daring to show his face in the light in case his story had somehow spread from Geneva. He stopped at taverns, sitting in the back, nursing a drink, listening to conversations in the hopes of hearing of a creature that haunts the woods. He heard nothing.

He went back to his old apartments and stood outside them.

Am I my creation's father? Was I wrong to abandon him? No, I was wrong in not destroying him.

Looking up to the window from which the creature had escaped, Victor looked towards the woods.

Then he felt it, the *frisson* of the bond between them. But it was different. Stronger. It called out to him. Returning to his present room, he retrieved what he had made, then walked into the woods, intent on finishing what he now believed should never have been started.

It was early morning when Adam Frankenstein awoke. "Do you feel that?"

"Yes, I do," Elizabeth replied. "But after last night …"

"No, I mean … Close your eyes, my Eve, reach out with your mind as I taught you." In preparation for this day, Adam trained Eve to be able to find him even when she could not see, hear, or smell him by casting her thoughts outwards and seek out the bond formed by the Elixir.

Her eyes closed and her brow furrowed. "Yes, I feel… a second presence. From you I feel love but from this weaker twin I feel … such hatred. Is it him?"

Adam nodded. "Yes, and he is close. Are you ready?"

"After what the hateful things he called me. After the brutality he inflicted on me. I will do what I must."

Adam kissed her. She responded but not as warmly as she had the night before. Then she had been intense and passionate. Now her lips were cold, her body stiff. *She is resolved*, he told himself.

One may walk quietly in the woods if one knows its ways. Victor did not. And while an ordinary human might not have heard his approach, Adam, his senses twice heightened by lightning, did.

They dressed and kissed again. Elizabeth departed, leaving

Adam alone.

Led by the bond between them, Victor found the cabin the creature had told him of. Suddenly the bond seemed to break apart and it was as if it were all around him.

What trickery is the beast up to, he wondered. One answer occurred to him but he rejected it, refusing to believe that his creation had the means or the intelligence to accomplish the task. Instead, he refused to believe his senses. Putting down his pack, he drew from it that which he had made in his room – glass bottles containing ignitable liquid and stoppered with rags soaked in oil.

As he approached the cabin, Adam's voice called out from inside.

"Good morning, Father. Have you come to talk? To settle things between us and so part in peace?"

"Foul thing, I have come to destroy you for all that you have taken from me."

Still concealing himself in the cabin, Adam said, "And you have taken from me."

"I cannot accept that, I will not accept that. You speak of peace. I care not for yours but for my own I do what I must."

One by one he put a flame to the rags and hurled the bottles, three in all, into the cabin. The glass broke, the liquid spread and burst into flame when it touched the fiery rags.

Victor watched as fire engulfed the cabin. He waited for the flames to drive the creature out so that he could throw the one remaining infernal device against his body and watch him burn. When his creation did not emerge, he listened for screams that never came.

So, the monster dies in silence, he thought, pleased with this ending. Then,

"Really, Father, did you not think that the cabin had a back door?"

Standing at a far enough distance away that he could easily dodge any throw from his father, Adam said, "Now you have taken my home, a home where I have twice known happiness. I ask again, let there be peace between us."

Angered by this deceit, Victor Frankenstein cried out, "To Hell with both of us." He moved to light the wick on his last device, planning on rushing his creation and immolating them both.

One may walk quietly in the woods if one knows its ways. Adam had shown this way to Elizabeth. She had left through the cabin's back door and, while Adam kept Victor engaged, had come around behind him. Victor, his senses only slightly more than human and mad for vengeance, did not sense her approach.

She waited for him to burn the cabin. Truth was, she was glad to see that shack, something she did not deem worthy of her, burn. She waited while Adam made his last appeal for peace and was glad to hear it rejected. When Victor moved to ignite his firebomb, she waited no longer.

There was hate within Elizabeth Frankenstein. There was hate for her uncle for exiling her mother. There was hate for her mother for bearing her. There was hate for the man she loved for bringing her back into low circumstances. And there was hate for the man who had many times abandoned her, who had used her, who had cursed her, and who had killed her. When the man who was once her husband cried out, "To Hell with both of us," and began to light the fuse, Elizabeth took this hate and used its strength to drive the sharp knife she carried through Victor Frankenstein's heart.

78

The bottle Victor had carried, the one with which he had meant to set fire to himself and his creation, fell harmlessly from his fingers to the ground, its fuse unlit. Elizabeth reached for it.

"What are you doing?" Adam asked.

"I plan to finish the job," she replied with bitter hatred. "I will burn his body so that he never returns."

Picking up the bottle, Adam shattered it against a large stone. "He never will. As long as the knife remains in his heart the elixir will work to revive him. Soon it will exhaust itself, his body will again become human and will decay.

"Eve," he said gently, trying to soothe her anger, "Victor Frankenstein was your cousin, your friend, and, for a very brief time, your husband and lover. In that he brought me into this life, he was my father. There are graves not far from here. Let us leave him with them. Let us leave him to rest in the peace he would not, could not accept in life."

Elizabeth thought on this for a while and finally said, "Very well. For the good times we shared, for his having made you and for the love we shared, I will let him rest in peace. And for his sins, I hope Dante's poem was more than a story and that he pays for them before finding this peace."

Close enough, Adam thought. Taking up his father's body, he buried it with the De Laceys, saying a prayer for all their souls, as well as his own if he had one.

They spent that night in his old cave. "We'll find better lodging tomorrow. Thanks to the coin I found in my father's pack, we can afford something worthy of you, for a time at least."

"About that, my Beast, now that Victor is dead ..."

Then she told Adam that she must return to Geneva, and why.

"Then we return to Geneva."

"No, Adam, not we. Me alone. You they would destroy. Without you, and with the way things are, they will have to take me in."

"And if they do not?"

To this question Elizabeth merely shrugged. "I do not know. I do know that I cannot live like this any longer, without a future and without a home. Right now, I need both."

Feeling the last of his happiness slip away, Adam sadly said, "I am sorry, Elizabeth. Not for loving you, for how could I not, but for not honoring your wishes to be with my father and become the Lady of House Frankenstein. I am sorry for doing to you what was done to me, calling you back to a life that was, as I see now, was not your own. Mostly I am sorry that I may never see you again."

As Elizabeth listened to her lover's words, her heart began to break. But she hardened it and without a word fell asleep in his arms for the last time.

In the morning she was gone.

79

Ernest Frankenstein was awakened by the cry of his servant, "Master Frankenstein, wake up. Come quickly. It's Lady Elizabeth, she's come back."

Ernest dressed and went down to find his sister-in-law standing in the entrance of the house. She was in a frightful state and he quickly ordered her taken in, allowed to bathe, given decent clothes to wear, and be fed breakfast. As this was being done, he summoned the authorities.

Magistrate Vernet responded and, together with Ernest, met with Elizabeth. After introductions were made and Elizabeth declined to have a female servant present as chaperone ("The fewer who hear the better") she told her story.

"Victor was the first man I knew in a carnal sense. As for his belief that there was another, well, like me, Victor was inexperienced. He did not know that accidents happen and that sometimes that which proves one's virtue gets damaged. He grew angry but before I could assure him of my love and fidelity, that … thing broke in. As a true husband should, Victor tried to defend me. He had earlier told me of threats made against him which is why there were pistols present. He wounded the monster, striking it. When the creature's blood splattered my breast, I fainted. It must have carried me away because when I awoke it was with me in some cave.

"Forgive my asking, Lady Frankenstein, but did this creature .. harm you … in any way."

Properly blushing, Elizabeth said, "Not in the way you mean, M. Vernet. It may not have been capable of such an act. I think it saw me as a sort of pet. It kept me prisoner, yes, but brought me food and water."

"Did it say anything?"

"No, Ernest, it could barely speak, just a few words such as 'Father' and 'Frankenstein' and sometimes 'Fire bad' when I asked it to start one."

"How did you escape?" Vernet asked, fascinated by her story.

"Victor found me. I do not know how but he did. He and the monster fought. He managed to slay it but at the cost of his own life. For what seemed like weeks I wandered lost in the forest. I managed to steal some clothing to cover my shame and it was only through God's grace that I found my way here."

Both Vernet and Ernest knew Victor's story, Vernet more than Ernest. Looking at each other, they nodded in silent agreement that Elizabeth's story was close enough to the truth to avoid further scandal. Ernest was about to accept her back into the House Frankenstein as his brother's widow.

"Is there anything else we should know, Elizabeth?" Ernest asked.

"Yes, there have been ... changes to my body. I believe I carry Victor's child, the heir to House Frankenstein."

This announcement creation some complications. Ernest was the appointed heir, but Elizabeth carried the rightful one. After some discussion, M. Vernet made a suggestion that was accepted by all.

A physician was called who verified Elizabeth's condition.

The bishop was called in. After some persuasion and a generous contribution to the church, a dispensation was granted.

There was a quick, private wedding uniting Ernest and Elizabeth in marriage. After a successful wedding night with no complaints from either party, Elizabeth took her place as mistress of House Frankenstein. And if from time to time she dreamed of a tall, not very handsome man with long black hair and pearly white teeth, that was no business of her husband.

ᏏᎧ

After he woke alone, Adam followed Elizabeth, tracking her movements through the elixir's bond until she arrived safely at the door of the Frankenstein manor. Then, with a whispered, "Fare you well, my Beauty, my Eve," he left her to the fulfillment of her dreams, hoping that that which she had so long desired would make her happy.

Then he returned to his father's grave.

Sometime later he stood on the hill on which he had called down the lightning and used his body to revive Elizabeth. There he dug a new grave and placed his father's body in it. From out of the grave rose a long metal rod, one end of which was in his father's heart in place of the knife Elizabeth had put there.

Adam was now alone. Alone except for the cat that had been following him since he had exhumed the body. It was the same cat who had often visited him in the past, the one whose fur now hid its scars, a cat he long ago realized he could sense before he could see. A cat who was very much like him.

Adam addressed his father.

"The elixir still flows through you, Father. Now that you are dead it may do the work for which it was intended. Perhaps your lungs are trying to draw air. Perhaps your heart is beating around the rod which impales it. If so, I give you this chance. Another chance of life, another chance at redemption, another chance to do right. There will come storms, and if Fate permits and my mother wishes, she will send to you her lighting and with it the spark of life. If so, make the best of your new life and if you seek me out may we be friends. Or it may be that you will lie here forever, some passerby having taken the rod to use as a walking stick. I have shown you what mercy I can, which is more than you deserve. Farewell, Father."

Having said goodbye to his father, Adam turned to the cat. He had long ago bonded with the small creature, the first being to willing touch him after his violent rebirth, one who taken to bringing him partially devoured tributes. Oddly, they were not just mice or marmots, but game as such as an Ibex or a bearded vulture, much larger than a typical cat should be able to hunt down.

"And what of the future, my friend. Will they tell stories of

Frankenstein and his monster? If so, what shape might they take? Perhaps my father will become a baron, or a doctor, or a madman in a castle. Or maybe I will be seen as a mindless monster who commits all sorts of murders, killing small children while befriending blind men? Who can say? Like my father's fate, such things are not in my control.

"But come, eh, Fritz, do you like Fritz? It was once my name and even creatures such as us deserve a name. Very well, Fritz it is. Let us leave this place and see where Fate might lead us."

The cat nodded as if it understood, then in a single leap landed on Adam's very large shoulder.

Adam looked out from the mountain and across the world that awaited him. A rare moment of peace came over him as he realized that, finally he was free of his father and free of his past. As he took his first step off the mountain and into his future, he was smiling and happy even though, behind him, storm clouds were gathering.

JOHN L. FRENCH is a retired crime scene supervisor with forty years' experience. He has seen more than his share of murders, shootings, and serious assaults. As a break from the realities of his job, he started writing science fiction, pulp, horror, fantasy, and, of course, crime fiction.

John's first story "Past Sins" was published in Hardboiled Magazine and was cited as one of the best Hardboiled stories of 1993. More crime fiction followed, appearing in Alfred Hitchcock's Mystery Magazine, the Fading Shadows magazines, and in collections by Barnes and Noble. Association with writers like James Chambers and the late, great C.J. Henderson led him to try horror fiction and to a still growing fascination with zombies and other undead things. His first horror story "The Right Solution" appeared in Marietta Publishing's Lin Carter's Anton Zarnak. Other horror stories followed in anthologies such as The Dead Walk and Dark Furies, both published by Die Monster Die books. It was in Dark Furies that his character Bianca Jones made her literary debut in "21 Doors," a story based on an old Baltimore legend and a creepy game his daughter used to play with her friends.

John's first book was The Devil of Harbor City, a novel done in the old pulp style. Past Sins and Here There Be Monsters followed. John was also consulting editor for Chelsea House's Criminal Investigation series. His other books include The Assassins' Ball (written with Patrick Thomas), Souls on Fire, The Nightmare Strikes, Monsters Among Us, The Last Redhead, the Magic of Simon Tombs, and When the Moon Shines. John is the editor of To Hell in a Fast Car, Mermaids 13, C. J. Henderson's Challenge of the Unknown, Camelot 13 (with Patrick Thomas), and (with Greg Schauer) With Great Power …

You can find John on Facebook or you can email him at him at jfrenchfam@ aol.com.

There has long been a debate among certain obscure and drunken literary scholars about whether **PATRICK THOMAS** was raised by Cthulhu, a leprechaun in a Manhattan bar, or two human parents. What there is no arguing about is that Patrick is the award-winning author of the beloved *Murphy's Lore* series and the darkly hilarious *Dear Cthulhu* advice empire and the creator of the *Agents of the Abyss* series.

His over 40 books include *Fairy with a Gun, By Darkness Cursed, Lore & Dysorder, Dead to Rites, Startenders, As the Gears Turn,* and *Exile & Entrance*. He is the co-author of the long running *Mystic Investigators* series and the Jack Gardner mysteries.

His latest series kicks off with *Bikini Jones Vs. The Brainnappers From Outer Space*. Patrick is the co-editor of *Camelot 13* (with John French), *New Blood* (with Diane Raetz), and *Hear Them Roar* (with CJ Henderson). He wrote the first two books in T*he Wildsidhe Chroncles* YA series. As **Patrick T. Fibbs**, he has penned the Ughabooz picture and first reader books as well as the middle reader books the Babe B. Bear Mysteries, the Undead Kid Diaries, and Joy Reaper Checks Out and the YA *Emotional Support Nightmare*.

Visit him online at www.patthomas.net and www.patricktfibbs.com.

DOWN THESE
MEAN STREETS
of Magic & Monsters walk the

MYSTIC INVESTIGATORS

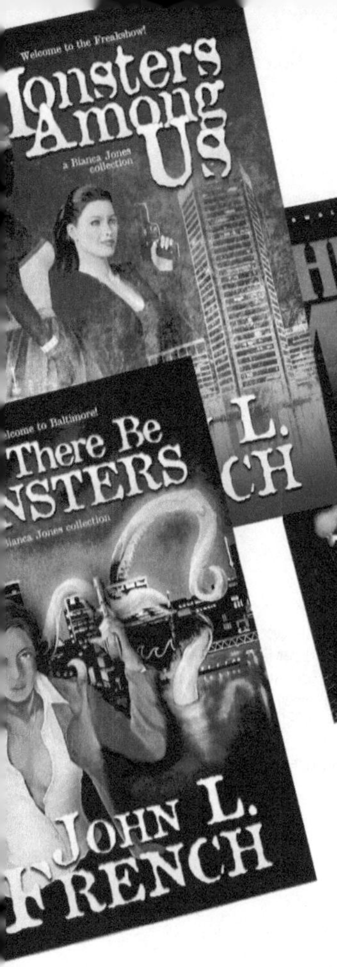

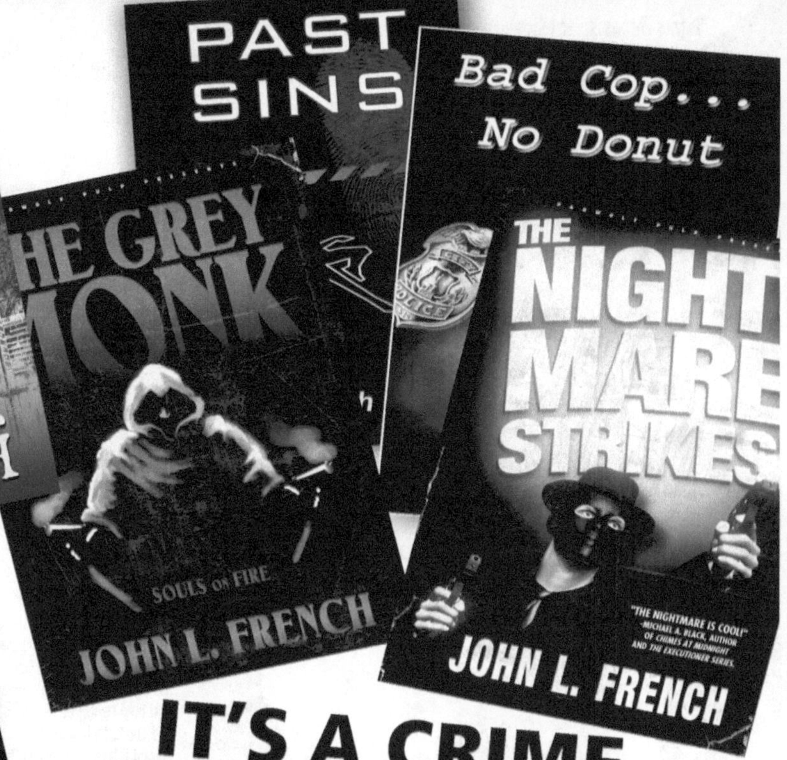

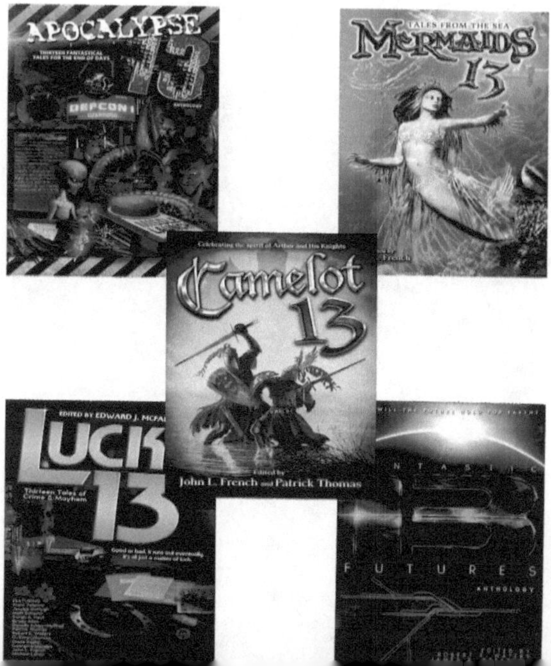

"Patrick Thomas is... so believable it's unbelievable."
-Ida Vega-Landow, The Journal of the Lincoln Heights Literary Society
DEAD TO RITES
Patrick Thomas
rites of Passage
John L. French
Patrick Thomas
When Darkness Falls
The Department of
Mystic Affairs
Picks up the pieces
From The Murphy's Lore Universe of
PATRICK THOMAS
www.patthomas.net
Find us on Facebook!

Fairy Rides The Lightning
PATRICK THOMAS

Fairy With A Gun
PATRICK THOMAS

Even the things that go Bump in the night
will learn that you DON'T mess with...
Terrorbelle
"Thomas certainly brings the goods to the table
when it comes to writing urban fiction...I promise, you will love...
Terrorbelle: Fairy With a Gun. Who doesn't love a well-stacked,
ass-kicking, gun-toting, woman with bullet-proof, razor-sharp wing
that investigates all manner of supernatural spookiness? I know
and Thomas's humor shows through in every tale. Jim Butcher an
Laurell K Hamilton have nothing on Thomas." The Raven's Barro
From The Murphy's Lore Universe of
PATRICK THOMAS

Shape up...
You only get
ONE Warning
Hell's Detective
No One Is Above The
Even

By Invocation Only
PATRICK THOMAS
Darkness CURSED
Hex marks the spot
PATRICK THOMAS

LORE & DYSORDER
PATRICK THOMAS
SHADOWS
CASE OF THE MOON MANIAC
"Dark... and charming."
- Ellen Datlow,
The Best Horror of the Year Vo

You can't keep a good man down
But you can KICK him off the planet!
PATRICK THOMAS

TALES OF STEAMWORLD
AS THE GEARS TURN
Grind 'Em!
PATRICK THOMAS
Steampunk Mayhem from the author of Murphy's Lore & Dear Cthulhu!
WWW.PATTHOMAS.NET
www.facebook.com/PatrickThomasAuthor

More GREAT Science Fiction!

"Delightfully Oddball"
-Dave Truesdale, SFSite
"Hilariously intelligent"
-Luke Reviews

CONSTELLATION PRIZE
PATRICK THOMAS

From behind the bar To Across The STARS
From The Murphy's Lore Universe of
PATRICK THOMAS
WWW.PATTHOMAS.NET
www.facebook.com/PatrickThomasAuthor

THE STARSCAPE PROJECT
As his quest begins, an artificial intelligence life form enters the galaxy and launches a series of covert attacks against the Empire. The Teconeans assume that the Federation is responsible, and galactic peace is about to unravel. As Stryker chases his nemesis into Teconean space, he finds himself thrown into the middle of the battle. Knowing that Earth will be the aliens' next target, Stryker must decide whether to let them destroy the Empire, or to join forces with his Teconean enemies against the invaders. The key to the mysterious aliens lies buried on the moon of Kennedy Prime, and it's up to Stryker to solve the puzzle before war begins. The fate of the galaxy is at stake.

THE STARSCAPE PROJECT
BRAD AIKEN

ZONE OF THE TENTH DEGREE
BRAD AIKEN

ZONE OF THE TENTH DGREE
1912, an alien ship crash lands in the Atlantic Ocean, setting up a secret colony that remains undetected for centuries, allowing them to manipulate some of the most important events in human history -- from the sinking of the Titanic to the Bermuda triangle to global warming. Now, the technology of the 26th century has uncovered the aliens' distress beacon, and it's a race against time as the Navy tries to stop a terrorist armed with a nuclear weapon from destroying the colony and triggering an all-out war as the mother-ship approaches

Now available from
PADWOLF
PUBLISHING

Help is only a Rainbow *Away*...

"Mix Gaiman's American Gods and Robinson's Callahan Crosstime Saloon on Prachett's Discworld and you get an idea of Thomas' Murphy's Lore." -David Sherman, author STARFIST and Demontech

"ENTERTAINING, INVENTIVE AND DELIGHTFULLY CREEPY." -JONATHAN MABERRY, New York Times and Bram Stoker Award Winning Author

"SLICK... ENTERTAINING Paul Di Filippo, ASIMOV'S

"HUMOR, OUTRAGEOUS ADVENTURES, & SOM CLEVER PLOT TWISTS." -Don D'Ammassa, SCIE FICTION CHRONICLE

PATRICK THOMAS

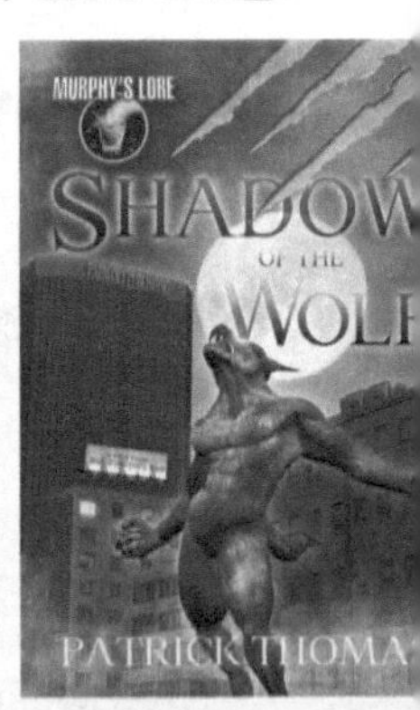